KID VS. SQUID

KID VS. SQUID

SQUID

GREG VAN EEKHOUT

BLOOMSBURY

NEW YORK BERLIN LONDON

First published in the United States of America in May 2010
by Bloomsbury Books for Young Readers
www.bloomsburykids.com

For information about permission to reproduce selections from this book, write to
Permissions, Bloomsbury BFYR, 175 Fifth Avenue, New York, New York 10010

Library of Congress Cataloging-in-Publication Data
Van Eekhout, Greg.
Kid vs. squid / by Greg van Eekhout. — 1st U.S. ed.
p.   cm.
Summary: Spending the summer after sixth grade at his great-uncle's oceanside
museum, Thatcher and local girl Trudy team up to help Shoal, one of the people of
Atlantis cursed by a witch whose head still survives, and who has an army of monstrous
creatures helping her.
ISBN 978-1-59990-489-4
[1. Imaginary creatures—Fiction. 2. Witches—Fiction. 3. Blessing and
cursing—Fiction. 4. Seashore—Fiction. 5. Atlantis (Legendary place)—Fiction.
6. Curiosities and wonders—Fiction.] I. Title. II. Title: Kid versus squid.
PZ7.V2744Kid 2010   [Fic]—dc22   2009036040

Book design by Donna Mark
Typeset by Westchester Book Composition
Printed in the U.S.A. by Worldcolor Fairfield, Pennsylvania
2 4 6 8 10 9 7 5 3 1

For Mama and Papa,
for giving me all those books
and raising me and stuff

KID vs. SQUID

CHAPTER 1

Dear Thatcher,
I'm off conducting some very important museum
business. Here's your to-do list. And remember,
a ship can't set sail without wind, so make
sure you eat something.
                              —Uncle Griswald

TO-DO LIST
1. *Water the plants*
2. *Feed Sinbad*
3. *Dust the shrunken heads*
4. *Clean the What-Is-It?? (but don't open the*
   box!!!)
5. *Have some lunch (pizza in fridge)*

So far I'd gotten as far as Number Two on Uncle
Griswald's list. Sinbad the tabby was lapping up

tuna-liver mix in my bedroom, which was really just a hammock in the closet where Griswald kept his mops and buckets. I tried not to mind so much. Believe me, there were worse places in the museum. For example, most of it. I couldn't even walk to the bathroom without passing a glass case containing four tiny severed heads with fins for ears. Dead-eyed, they grinned fiercely, daring me to touch them with my feather duster.

Me, Thatcher Hill, versus the shrunken heads. This was my summer vacation.

I was supposed to be spending the time between sixth and seventh grades traveling through Asia with my parents. They owned the biggest squirt gun distributorship in Arizona, and they were touring overseas squirt gun factories in exotic and interesting places. But one of my classmates had caught some kind of kangaroo rat virus, and even though I didn't get sick, I was exposed and wasn't allowed to travel out of the country. I'd begged my folks to let me stay with friends in Phoenix, but they decided I should be watched by family. My closest relative was Mom's uncle, my great-uncle Griswald, so they shipped me off to live with him in Los Huesos, California.

I'll have plenty more to say about Los Huesos later. Right now, I want to tell you about Uncle Griswald's museum.

Maybe you've been to a museum on a school field trip. Maybe there were dinosaurs or old paintings or statues of naked people inside. Griswald's museum wasn't like that. Professor Griswald's Museum of the Strange and Curious and Gift Emporium sat crammed on the Los Huesos boardwalk between a hot dog stand and a tattoo parlor. Here, Griswald displayed things that looked like they'd been dredged up from a deep ocean trench where all the ugliest sea creatures live because it's dark and nobody has to look at them there. He had a fish with a green handlebar mustache in a jar. He had a hand with suction cups and eyeballs. And a thing that looked half-fish and half-monkey, labeled the Feejee Mermaid. A tiny, withered man with pants made of sardines. An octopus with sneakers on the ends of its eight arms. The shrunken heads. And so forth.

He even kept a mummy in a glass-lidded sarcophagus, resting on a pair of sawhorses. It was the color of beef jerky, with dark black squiggles down its arms that looked like sea horses. Griswald said the squiggles were tattoos. I thought they were done in Magic Marker. The mummy had no head. Mummies *with* heads cost a lot. He'd found this one washed up on the beach, which was his favorite way to acquire exhibits, since it was free.

Places like my uncle's used to be called dime

museums, because marks (another word for "customers," or "suckers") were charged a dime to gawk. Uncle Griswald charged three dollars.

I gave the shrunken heads a quick pass with my feather duster and moved on to the *What-Is-It??*

So, what was it?

It was a barnacle-encrusted wooden box with swirly grain that reminded me of ocean waves. One side had a window of bubbly green glass, and through the glass, you could almost see a face looking back at you: pale eyelids, a sharp blade of a nose, and a wide, thin-lipped mouth turned down in a grimace. Griswald said it was a very important head, but he couldn't remember exactly what made it so important. He'd had an accident of some kind a while back, and it had messed him up in a lot of ways, his memory included.

I smacked the feathers of my duster against the box a few times and wiped the glass with a damp cloth. The museum was now as ready for visitors as it ever would be, but so far this morning, nobody had walked past the door, much less come inside.

According to the to-do list, it was time for lunch. I went to the fridge in Uncle Griswald's cramped little kitchen and excavated a take-out pizza box from beneath two six-packs of beer. Normally the thought of cold pizza would fill me with a sense of joy and wonder, because if there's a more perfect food than pizza, it's *cold* pizza. But this pizza was made of evil. The cheese resembled the inside of an orange peel. The toppings looked like something left behind by seagulls.

I closed the box.

"Aren't you going to eat that?"

Leaning on a crutch, Griswald filled the kitchen doorway. He looked like a cartoon sailor, with a wind-burned red face fringed by a white beard. Taking in his black wool cap and matching sweater, I figured he'd probably been out throwing harpoons at whales. I still didn't know what had happened to his left leg, but half of it wasn't there.

"I'm not hungry this morning, I guess."

He gave me a look that I didn't know how to read. He'd never been married and wasn't used to having kids around, and I wasn't used to spending time with crusty old mariners.

"Well, all right," he said. "If you're not going to eat it—"

I thrust the pizza box at him, grateful when he took it from my hands.

"I'm done dusting the exhibits," I said. "I thought I'd take a walk out in the cold, damp air."

Griswald nodded thoughtfully, his jaw working on

balsa-wood pizza crust. "It's a fine day for it. But if you comb the beach, watch your step. Lots of wickedness on the shore this time of year."

"Wickedness? You mean like toxic syringes?"

He was about to answer my question, but then seemed to forget what he was going to say. "Just be careful."

I left the museum behind and headed down the boardwalk. Perched on the edge of a crumbling sandstone cliff above the beach, the boardwalk was a half-mile strip of weathered planks, possibly salvaged from a pirate ship. T-shirt shops and pizza stands and other touristy joints stretched out into the fog. Almost all of them were shuttered and closed. Even though it was the first week of June, the tourists still hadn't arrived.

I leaned over the guardrail and looked down across the beach. This was not a golden-sand, volleyball-net, bikini-girls kind of beach. This was more of a rocky, driftwood, kelpy kind of beach. Not a place where you'd slather yourself with sunblock and lay out on a towel with a paperback book. For one thing, the smell of rotting seaweed would detract from your enjoyment. Also, you'd have to share space with a lot of dead fish. Everything the ocean couldn't stomach washed up on this beach.

Los Huesos was Spanish for "the bones," and the

town was built on a huge slab of rock that jutted out to sea like a broken middle finger, flipping off the Pacific Ocean. Offshore, scattered boulders stood like the guano-glazed vertebrae of a giant.

I turned away from the rail to find I was being watched.

Two guys about my size sat on BMX bikes in front of the shut-down saltwater taffy stand. They wore hoodies with the hoods up, their faces hidden behind big sunglasses and bandannas.

"Hey," I said, raising my hand in a dorky little wave.

They didn't reply. They didn't move. Their gloved hands gripped the handlebars of their bikes. It was a cold day, but not worth bundling up for. Maybe they had some condition that made them sensitive to sunlight.

Wordlessly, they pedaled the few yards over to me until their knobby front tires almost touched my shins. My legs told me to run, but I wasn't going to listen to my wussy legs. I'd had six months of tae kwon do training when I was nine. I'd made it to green belt.

"You wanna back off a bit?" I said, trying to make it sound less like a request and more like a threat. Unfortunately, tough-guy talk had never been my biggest strength. I'm more jokey than punchy-kicky. Jokes are my armor.

Back in elementary school everyone knew me, and

I knew everyone, and they called me by my first name, and I called everyone by their first names. That was the natural way of things in elementary school. But there's nothing natural about middle school. Middle school is just a very unnatural place. It's too big, a landfill where all the kids graduating from nine elementary schools get dumped. Instead of a few hundred classmates, I have a couple thousand. In elementary school I was Thatcher. In middle school, I'm a last name.

Middle school made me funny-mean. My mouth started getting me in trouble. I respond to bullies and teachers with funny comments, sharp little put-downs, and sometimes if my victim shows signs of weakness, I can't stop myself. My words are like a cheetah taking down a gazelle by the throat.

These weird guys didn't seem like gazelles.

"Are you flotsam?" one of them said in a slushy voice. It sounded like he needed to swallow. Let's call him Left.

"Am I *what*sam?"

The other one, Right, pulled a small book from his pocket. The cover was made of two clam shells, joined by a hinge. "He can't be flotsam," Right gurgled. "He's not in the book."

"We've never seen you before, so you're not a townie," said Left.

"But since you're not in the book, you can't be flotsam," said Right.

"We're done here," Left said to his brother or friend or co-freak. "But we'll be watching you."

With that, they turned their handlebars, and when they did, the cuff of Left's sleeve rode up and I caught a brief glimpse of his wrist. The skin was white and shiny. A little bit transparent. I could see thin black veins branching below his flesh. I thought of an entire arm that looked like that, a face that looked like that, and I tried to stop thinking about it, because it was making me kind of sick to my stomach.

"I'll be watching you watching me," I said, this time with a *deliberately* dorky wave. The boys popped wheelies and rode off.

🐚

Later, back at the museum, Griswald and I were having dinner. And by dinner, I mean Wonder bread and some kind of cheese substance that sprayed from a can. Sitting at a folding card table, Griswald told me about his day, which mostly involved searching the thrift shop downtown for used sneakers. "For the octopus," he explained.

"What's wrong with the sneakers it's wearing?"

"Everybody deserves fresh sneakers," Griswald said, very seriously.

"And I suppose being a cephalopod who lives in a jar doesn't change that."

"Exactly," he said, wiping cheese substance from his mouth with a paper towel. "Did you have a good walk?"

"I did. I smelled a lot of kelp."

"Excellent. Did anything interesting happen?" He made it sound like a casual question, but I could tell there was something he *wasn't* asking, as if he was worried what my answer might be.

I thought about the weird guys on the bikes. And I thought about my great-uncle, sitting across the rickety table from me, whose biggest concern was buying shoes for a pickled octopus.

"No," I said. "Nothing interesting."

"Ah."

I couldn't tell if he was disappointed or relieved.

"May I have some more cheese spray, please?"

That night, curled up in my hammock as Sinbad nested in my suitcase, I dreamed of jellyfish. They stared down on me with almost-human eyes.

CHAPTER 2

I awoke hours before sunrise in the dark, with the remnants of my dreams still clinging like suction cups. The museum made noises as I lay suspended in my hammock. During the day, the place was just goofy, a few rooms of exhibits made from papier-mâché and modeling clay. The Feejee Mermaid was obviously a monkey torso of cardboard and rabbit fur sewn on to a leather fish tail. Fakes like that were called "gaffs," and they weren't scary in sunlight.

Night was different. Wood creaked. Ice clinked in the refrigerator. Air whispered through the water pipes, sounding almost like voices. It figured: what's the point of living in a creepy museum if it doesn't get even creepier at night?

I thought about my parents on the other side of the globe. Internet and phone service in Los Huesos stank, so Mom and Dad sent me the occasional post-card, mostly about the squirt gun business: *Dear Thatcher, We think we've found a great deal on polymer injection molds. Love and huggies.*

I wondered if my friends back in Phoenix missed me. Everyone was doing fine, I supposed.

As if sensing my unease, Sinbad hopped into my hammock and sat on my stomach, purring as I scratched his scruff. He was a pretty fat cat, so I wasn't exactly comfortable with his weight pressing on me, but at least he made me feel less alone. After a while, I started drifting back to sleep.

Then glass shattered.

I shot up in my hammock. Sinbad hissed in protest and leaped off me.

Holding my breath, I listened.

Nothing.

Maybe I'd just dreamed the sound.

But then I heard footsteps. Too light to be the clomp of Griswald's crutch. This was the sound of someone creeping along in the dark. I imagined white, slimy feet trailing seawater.

Another noise came from the museum. A thump, a rattle, a jiggle. I wasn't imagining it; there was definitely someone out there.

Was Griswald awake? Did he know we had an

intruder? Was he even home, or was he out drinking with his salty old cronies at the Shipwreck Tavern?

As quietly as I could, I lowered myself from my hammock and put my ear to the door.

The door between me and the hallway was just a flimsy sliding panel, but it suddenly seemed like a brick wall, something that would keep me safe if only I kept it closed. But what if the prowler outside was a serial killer, and what if Griswald *was* home, and while I cowered in my room, he was getting murdered?

"Did you have a nice vacation?" Mom and Dad would ask at the end of summer.

And I would have to answer back, "Yeah, it was great. Uncle Griswald got his throat slit while I hid with the cat. I ate cheese spray for dinner."

I slid the door open a crack.

I could still hear the wincing squeak of floorboards. It no longer sounded like lurking. It sounded purposeful. Like someone searching.

Tiptoeing down the hall, I reached Griswald's room and peered inside. His door stood open, the bed empty. He'd left me alone with a human-jellyfish-hybrid murdering psychopath. Or at least a burglar.

Something bumped my leg, and I choked off a startled scream as Sinbad streaked by in a flash of fur. An instant later, I heard someone else choke off their own startled scream from the dark exhibit room.

I ran into the museum.

The intruder wasn't a jellyfish boy. It was a thin girl, staring at me with sharp, glittering eyes. Her ears were swept back, almost pointed. Bits of shattered door glass clung to the tattered tails of her black raincoat. In her golden brown, long-fingered hands, she clutched the *What-Is-It??*

"Hey!" was the most brilliant thing I could think of to say.

She hissed at me, baring her teeth, and darted out the door.

I gave chase, out the museum, down the boardwalk, my bare feet slapping hard against the wooden planks. Wet ocean air chilled me through the thin fabric of my T-shirt and pajama pants.

The girl made good speed, but I was a pretty decent runner. I had lots of experience running from mean dogs and bullies who weren't amused by my smart mouth or impressed by my tae kwon do belt.

The girl's raincoat flapped as she ran down two flights of wooden steps to the beach. I raced after her, hoping not to spear the soles of my feet with splinters. Upon reaching the bottom of the stairs, she jetted down the beach. The tide was in, but she expertly dodged the surf and scrambled across slick rocks and jagged pieces of driftwood.

"Hey!" I called out again. "That's my *What-Is-It??*!"

She didn't seem to care. She kept on running.

Uttering bad words, I picked my way across the jumbled shoreline. Something stabbed my foot. I'd stepped on a rock. Or maybe a shellfish. I was sure I'd broken the skin. I would probably bleed to death now, or at least contract some sort of rare crustacean disease. My whole leg would swell up to the size of a blimp. It would turn orange and purple and grow suction cups. Doctors would cut it off and Griswald would put it in a big jar and charge people three bucks to see it.

I limped on for a while more, blood seeping between my toes, but it was no good. The girl was too far ahead.

I watched her move nimbly over the obstacle course until she vanished in a nest of boulders.

Now I'd never find out what the *What-Is-It??* was. I didn't know why that should bother me so much, but it did.

Wet and shivering, I dragged myself back to the boardwalk.

At Griswald's I treated my foot with rubbing alcohol, gauze, and more bad words. Sinbad kept trying to lick my toes. Either he wanted to comfort me, or he was a vampire cat. I swept up the shattered glass and replaced the broken pane with cardboard and duct tape. Just as I was putting away the tape, Uncle Griswald came home. It was four thirty in the morning.

His bloodshot eyes went wide as he took in the crime scene. "What happened?"

"Burglar. Juvenile delinquent. The *What-Is-It??* is gone."

Griswald said bad words of his own. I'd heard all of them before, but never in that combination.

He conducted a full inspection of the museum and found nothing else missing. The Mustache Fish and Little Mister Fishy Pants and the cash box all remained in their proper places.

With a frown, he scratched his beard. "Why steal the *What-Is-It??* unless it's valuable?" he muttered to himself. "Valuable or . . . important." He looked more and more miserable as he thought about it. "If only I could remember . . ." It was only then that he noticed my bandaged foot. "Did you cut yourself on the glass?"

I shook my head and told him how I'd chased the girl.

Griswald whistled through his teeth. "That was foolhardy, Thatcher. Foolhardy, but very brave."

"It wasn't brave. She was short and skinny. She

was practically dressed in rags. I should have just called the cops."

But Griswald let out a bitter laugh. "Wouldn't have done us any good, lad. It takes more than a break-in to spur the police into action around here. I don't know what it would take."

I was cold and tired and my foot throbbed and I wanted to be back home in Phoenix. If Griswald didn't want to report the burglary, fine. It wasn't my business. It wasn't my decapitated head.

"I'm going back to bed," I announced, and I returned to my hammock. Hanging there like exhausted laundry, I closed my eyes and tried not to listen to the air whispering through the pipes.

Stupid pipes.

Stupid air.

I could have sworn they were saying "Flotsam."

CHAPTER 3

Griswald stayed in the next morning, and he was still snoring when I woke up. Since he hadn't left me a to-do list, I felt free to venture outside before dusting the devil fish and the snorkel dog. After giving Sinbad a blob of canned meat, I headed out the door.

The boardwalk had come alive.

A pair of little girls with pigtails led their mom into the candy shop and came out with pink plumes of cotton candy.

Tattoo guns buzzed inside the tattoo parlor.

"You smell that, son?" called a man from a popcorn cart. Chemical butter odors wafted on the air. "That's the smell of the sea, and the sea says you need popcorn."

"Maybe later," I muttered. "But let me ask you something. Why'd everybody suddenly show up today?"

He was broad-shouldered, in a too-small T-shirt with a faded crown on the front. A beard of silver curls blended with the mane of hair spilling down his shoulders. His eyes were the color of coal, and they suddenly grew sharp and furious. I stepped back, wondering what I'd said to make him angry. But then his look softened. He seemed to get sleepy, and he blinked.

"You smell that, son?"

"The sea?"

"It's the smell of the sea, and the sea says you need popcorn."

"Didn't we just have this conversation?"

"You smell that, son?"

"Ah, yes, the smell of repetition."

Stumbling along with my sore foot, I left him and his smell behind.

A partially dismantled Ferris wheel stood farther down the boardwalk behind a plywood fence. Curious, I used an abandoned plastic paint pail for a boost and pulled myself up to peer at the wreck. It towered over a dry moat—maybe the former home of alligators or piranhas—that was now just a muddy trench. Buckets for riders dangled off the wheel like loose teeth. I didn't think I'd be riding it anytime this summer.

Next to the Ferris wheel, a train of roller-coaster

cars ratcheted up the hill. The train wasn't full, but the few passengers let out impressive screams as the cars swooshed down.

Merchants arranged T-shirts and beach towels in front of their shops. A woman at the bike and skate rental pumped air into bicycle tires. Beeps and buzzers sounded from the arcade. A man on a bench threw seed at a mob of pigeons.

Where had all these people suddenly come from?

A girl approached me.

"You look confused."

Solidly built, she stood a couple inches taller than me, with an FBI Academy baseball cap jammed over a head of tight black curls. Lively brown eyes stared from her dark brown face. I felt like I was being studied and judged.

"It's First Day," she said, sweeping her hand over her head to indicate the entire boardwalk. "It happens like this every year. One day, ghost town, the next day, all this."

"The same day every year?" I asked.

"Walk with me," she said. Adjusting the backpack she wore slung over one shoulder, she started down the boardwalk toward the midway without waiting for any response from me. I followed.

"Last year First Day happened in July," she went on. "I heard it was late May the year before that, one of the earliest First Days ever, but I wasn't there for it. I moved here a week before First Day last year."

"There wasn't anyone here yesterday. Do the shop people and tattoo artists and everyone live in town?"

"Some do, but not many. Most of the workers just sort of roll in on First Day, like flotsam on the waves."

That word again. The jellyfish boys had asked if I was flotsam. Was she friends with them? If so, I didn't think I wanted to know her. But except for Griswald and his tabby cat, I'd had no one to talk to in weeks. So I kept walking with the girl.

"Flotsam," I said. "What does that word mean?"

"You know, the floating wreckage of a ship. As opposed to jetsam, which is what gets tossed overboard to lighten the load during a storm."

Jetsam. Kind of like how my parents had tossed me to Griswald to lighten their load.

As we continued along, merchants and snack vendors watched us go by. I didn't like the way their eyes tracked us, not even bothering to hide the fact that they were staring. Maybe they were just hungry for our business.

The girl offered her hand. "I'm Trudy McGee, by the way."

We shook. She had a strong grip. "I'm Thatch—"

"Thatcher Hill," she interrupted. "I know. You're Griswald's nephew." And then, before I could say anything, she corrected herself. "Great-nephew, I mean. So, I heard you had some excitement at the museum last night."

"Guess word gets around fast in Los Huesos. Griswald said he wasn't going to bother with a police report. He said the cops around here aren't very motivated."

She smiled a little. "Some things get around fast. Other things don't get around at all. Did the thief get anything good?"

"Just the *What-Is-It??* And before you ask, I don't know what it is. Could be a genuine human head. Could be a mummified honeydew melon."

"That's all he took? No cash? No valuables?"

"Just that. And the thief was a she. About our age, I'd guess, or a little younger."

Trudy gave me a laser-focused look. "You saw her?"

"Yeah," I said, going on to describe my hot-foot pursuit.

Trudy stopped at the rail overlooking the beach. I stood beside her. The tide was out, leaving the broad, debris-strewn beach exposed.

"This is a very curious case of breaking and entering," she said, more to herself than to me. "Not the typical burglar profile for Los Huesos. And taking something of little or no value? It doesn't make sense. Unless," Trudy added, turning to face me, "the *What-*

Is-It?? does have value. You say you lost her on the beach?"

"Yeah, in the rocks. Why are you so interested in the break-in?"

"I'm a busybody," she said, all business.

She took off down a rickety set of wooden steps to the beach and moved briskly over rocks and sand. Limping on my sore foot, I struggled to keep up, navigating around piles of kelp until I caught up with her at the bird-poop-splattered rocks where I'd lost the girl-thief. Shallow waves smacked against them, even at low tide. Between two of the largest rocks was a narrow, half-submerged tunnel opening.

"Ready to get wet?" Trudy asked.

"What, you want to go in?"

She looked at me, eyes wide in disbelief. "You *don't?* The thief stole something from your own uncle."

"*Great*-uncle. And like I said, he didn't even call the cops. Besides, all she made off with was some nasty piece of junk. One less thing for me to dust."

I thought she'd argue with me, but she just shrugged.

"Okay, Thatcher. Nice meeting you. Maybe I'll see you later." With that, she removed her shoes and stowed them in her backpack before splashing into the foamy seawater.

If she'd said it angrily, or snottily, I probably

would have let her go. But she didn't seem to care one way or the other if I went with her, as if none of this really concerned me, as if I was a bystander, free to involve myself in the mystery of the *What-Is-It??* heist or not.

I thought back to the jellyfish boys. They'd asked if I was flotsam.

Somehow, I'd become involved in *something*.

CHAPTER 4

I took off my shoes, rolled up my jeans, and stepped into the churning, cold water. When I looked down I couldn't see my feet. I thought about stingrays. Did they even have stingrays in this part of the world? I remembered hearing the best way to treat a stingray sting was to pee on it, but I couldn't remember if that meant you were supposed to pee on the stingray or on where you got stung. You know you're having a bad summer vacation when you're trying to remember if you should pee on yourself.

We paused at the tunnel opening in the rocks. Water soaked me up to my waist.

"I can't see anything," I said. "It's too dark."

"Got it covered," Trudy said, taking a flashlight from her backpack.

This wasn't just any flashlight. Black steel with

a textured barrel, it was a serious instrument. She switched it on and a sharp white beam lit the tunnel.

"C'mon," she said.

I sloshed after her through the entrance. The ceiling of jagged rock dipped so low we had to bend over double to avoid scraping our heads. Mussels lined the walls, like thousands of crusty blackbird beaks. The moist air reeked of fish.

The tunnel veered right and continued on, farther than I'd hoped, stretching beyond the reach of Trudy's flashlight.

"What are we looking for, exactly?" I asked her. "The girl's secret thief headquarters?"

"Indications," Trudy said. "Signs."

A wave came in and pushed seawater into my face. I wondered how many unanswered postcards it would take for my parents to learn I'd drowned. With brine draining from my nose, I kept going.

The tunnel ended in a slit between two rocks, just wide enough for Trudy and me to squeeze through one at a time. We came out in a cove surrounded by sandstone cliffs. On a lip of sand before us, a boat the size of a convenience store lay on its side. It might have been white once, but now it was mottled with rust and green algae.

"So would you call that a boat or a ship?" I asked Trudy.

"I'd call it awfully suspicious. Those cliffs are too steep and crumbly to climb, and anyone who tries to swim out of this cove is asking to get dashed against the rocks. Conclusion: there's a good chance our thief is hiding inside."

I thought there was a good chance Trudy was the weirdest person I'd met in Los Huesos so far. And that included Griswald and the BMX guys.

On the other hand, there was a chance she was right, and if I wasn't going to have a bikini-girls kind of summer, I'd need some kind of adventure to make up for it.

We splashed through pooled water and peered through a gap in the ship's hull into the dark interior. Trudy shined her flashlight beam inside. I'd expected to see a jumble of nets and boaty things, all tossed about on their sides. But everything had been cleared off and neatly stacked against the interior hull. A set of sandy footprints, smaller than my own, led off deeper into the ship. We were on the right track.

"Come on," Trudy said, squeezing through the gap into the boat.

The trail of footprints took us through what I guessed was the engine room, filled with pipes and machinery that had to be crawled over or ducked under, or, sometimes, knocked with my head. A lot of it was green with ocean muck and encrusted with barnacles.

Trudy shoved her flashlight in her pocket and took a disposable camera from her backpack. As I poked the walls with my finger, she snapped off shots.

"Careful where you aim that," I said, blinking bright spots from my eyes. "What are you doing, anyway?"

"Documenting for later analysis."

"Documenting for . . . ?"

"Sorry. Me take pictures so me can look at later. Better?"

"Yes, a little bit. How long do you think the wreck's been here?"

"It shouldn't be here at all," said Trudy. "A wreck this size ought to be listed in the historical records, and this one isn't."

"You're a history buff." I'd heard of such people, but had never met one.

"My mom owns the secondhand bookstore on Main Street. She bought it last year, complete with stock. The old owner left behind boxes of old maps and books about Los Huesos history. I've at least paged through most of them."

"History buff," I said again, this time with more conviction.

She peered at the wall with a powerful little

magnifying glass. "History is a weapon that helps me understand Los Huesos. And I will use every weapon in my arsenal."

I actually liked the way Trudy talked. She reminded me of Batman.

Which I guess made me Robin.

Nobody wants to be Robin.

Just then a hideous growl echoed through the cabin. It was like a force of nature, deep and low and gurgly and unlike any beast I could imagine.

It was my stomach.

"Sorry," I whispered. "I skipped breakfast."

Trudy dug in her backpack and handed me a little plastic sandwich bag. It contained a sugar-glazed doughnut. "Eat it before your stomach gives us away."

I accepted the doughnut and looked upon Trudy with a little bit of awe. I couldn't help but be impressed with her. Even Batman didn't carry doughnuts.

After making the doughnut disappear in three bites, I wiped my sugary fingers on my pants and continued on with Trudy.

The footprints came up to a closed hatch, and now I got nervous. There's something unsettling about opening closed doors without knowing what's on the other side. But that's what we'd come here to do. I bent down and pushed open the hatch cover.

We crawled through into a cramped compartment, barely more than a closet, with a closed door on the other side. Mouthwatering smells of garlic and ginger and hot spices wafted over me. The walls were lined with shelves bearing bags of shrimp chips and flounder jerky, as well as jars containing fish the size of pocket combs, little squids and octopuses, and other, odder, pale creatures that looked as if they'd been dredged up from the same place as the exhibits in Griswald's museum.

"Somebody spends a lot of time here," Trudy whispered. "Clearly, we've discovered our criminal's secret lair."

And from the sounds of slurping I could hear coming from the other side of another narrow door, someone was home. I'd had enough skulking about. Through the door I went, and into a small galley with a sink, stove, and cupboards. Sitting at a table, drinking soup from a Thermos cup, was the thief from the night before. The *What-Is-It??* rested at her elbow beside salt and pepper shakers.

"Hey!" I shouted, rushing into the galley. "That's my . . . thing!" I lunged for the *What-Is-It??*, startling the girl, but she recovered quickly. Grabbing the box and tucking it under her arm, she slid away from the table. The blade of a knife glinted in her hand.

"Back off, land-dweller," she hissed.

I couldn't place her accent. French? Chinese? Minnesotan? I'm not good with accents. Anyway, I was more focused on her knife.

Trudy flipped open a notebook. She clicked a pen. "Your name, permanent address, and legal guardian, please?"

"Attempt to wrest the head from me and I'll gut you, girl," snarled the thief.

Trudy wrote something down and said, "You can try."

The thief only smiled.

Things were getting a little crazy, what with the snarling and the threats and the knife. I wanted the *What-Is-It??* back, but I wasn't sure a potential head-in-a-box was worth all this.

Hoping to relieve the tension in the room, I cleared my throat and tried to think of a good distracting knock-knock joke.

Then, behind me, someone else coughed. Not Trudy, not the girl-thief. This was a wet, shlurpy cough. "Ah, it's the museum boy and the bookstore girl and Shoal the Flotsam," a familiar voice said. "Give us the box, or we will kill you."

The BMX boys weren't wearing their bandannas and sunglasses like they had on the beach, so I saw the white, oozy flesh of their faces. I saw their shiny black eyes, no bigger than dimes. Where their mouths should have been were puckered seams. It was as if they'd been interrupted while morphing from human to jellyfish.

One of the jellies rushed me, his bare hands the color of snot.

"Don't let them touch you!" Shoal screamed.

Before I could react, she jumped up on the table and used it as a launching pad to hurl herself at the jellies. She howled like a rabid cat, and the jellies ducked and dodged, trying to avoid her slicing knife. The small space became an insane riot of flying fists and elbows and sharp objects. A jelly dove at me, and Shoal was there again, warding him off with slashing motions of her knife.

"Leave the land-dwellers alone," she said in a commanding voice. Unfortunately, in the crowded confines, her blade was just as much a threat to me as it was to the jelly, and I came within an inch of losing an ear. But at least she was trying to defend me.

I caught a glimpse of Trudy from the corner of my eye. She faced off with the other jelly, brandishing her flashlight like a mighty club. I made a mental note: next time I went poking my nose into danger, I would come better prepared with a weapon of some kind and maybe some batarangs.

I hurried to the drawer by the sink, anxious to get my hands on a steak knife, at least. Grabbing the first thing available, I spun to face my opponent. He shlurped a laugh. Looking down, I saw that I was trying to threaten him with a potato peeler.

Abandoning the peeler, I found a rolling pin and brought it down on the jelly's head.

"Hey!" he shlobbed. "Ow!"

I bashed him again. He lunged away but then spun back toward me, his white palm coming at my face in an openhanded slap. Shoal was there in a blur, shoving me aside and taking the slap intended for me across her cheek. It didn't seem like that strong of a blow, just a glancing strike, but Shoal dropped as if she'd been smashed by a hammer. She writhed on the ground, struggling for breath, her eyes rolling so far back that all I could see were the whites.

She looked like she was dying.

CHAPTER 5

Still wielding my rolling pin, I moved between Shoal and the jellyfish boy who'd slapped her. "What did you do to her?"

His green white fingers jittered, ink black veins under the skin. "I stung her," he said.

"And now we're taking the witch's head with us," said the other jelly. "Try to stop us, and we'll sting you again and again and again. That'll be fun."

Trudy knelt by Shoal, trying to keep her still as she flailed, clawing at the floor.

I grabbed the *What-Is-It??* and shoved it at the jellies. "Here, take it and get lost."

One of the jellies snatched it away from me and cradled it in his weird hands. "We'll see you again!" they gurgled, taking off through the hatch.

"Go eat sand!" I shouted to their retreating

footsteps. I wanted to chuck the rolling pin at their heads, but better to get them out of here so we could help Shoal. They could have the stupid head in a box, for all I cared. It seemed to be important to Shoal, but now her life was at stake.

"How is she?" I said, joining Trudy at Shoal's side.

"She's not breathing well, and her lips and tongue are swollen. I think she's in anaphylactic shock."

Shoal's breaths came in a high, weak whistle.

Back home I had a friend who was allergic to fish, only he didn't know it until Bring a Weird Snack to School Day. He had to be carted away by paramedics after taking a bite from a patty smelt. Anaphylactic shock became the unofficial vocabulary item of the day.

I dug my phone out of my pocket to call 911. There were zero bars. "I'm not getting a signal."

"I'll try mine," said Trudy. But she didn't have any better luck than me.

"Maybe getting them wet fritzed them out."

"Impossible. My backpack's waterproof."

Shoal's hand shot out and grabbed my arm.

"Pantry," she gasped. "Silver shell."

"What—"

"Silver shell," she croaked. "Cure."

I raced into the pantry and searched the shelves, passing up jars containing fish with tentacles, fish with three heads, a sea horse with a human-looking face, a tiny creature that looked like a smaller version of Griswald's Feejee Mermaid . . . and then I found it: a jar with a thing that looked like a hot dog with beady little eyes, covered in a silver, mirror-bright shell.

I brought the jar with the hot dog–fish into the kitchen and unscrewed the lid. Dipping my hand inside, I pulled it out. I could see my face reflected in its silver surface. I looked very freaked out.

"I've got the fish, Shoal. What do I do with it?"

Shoal's eyelids fluttered, her flesh the color of a dirty tube sock. Somehow, I felt responsible for what was happening to her. I didn't want her to die.

"Shoal! Hey! Talk to me!"

She said something, but I couldn't understand it. I leaned in closer. "Come on, Shoal. Help us."

"Feed me," she said, her words garbled and thick.

I touched the fish to Shoal's lips. With a jerky twist of her neck, she bit down, tearing the fish's head off. She struggled to chew, nostrils flaring to draw in air. Eyes wide open in pain or panic, she forced the chewed-up head down her throat. I was sure she'd choke. But after a moment, the tension in her arched back relaxed. Her color improved and she seemed to breathe a little easier.

Eventually, she was able to sit slumped against the cupboards, knees drawn into her chest. Trudy gave her some water from a bottle she had in her backpack, but Shoal didn't seem grateful. She glared at Trudy and me as if we were the ones who'd stung her. "Give me the head."

"Can't," I said. "I gave it to the jellies."

"You *what*? What kind of crab-brained fool are you?" Shoal tried to stand but only managed to get her butt a few inches off the ground before sagging back down.

"Hey, don't get all insulty on me. The head didn't belong to you in the first place. I gave away property you stole because I wanted to get rid of the jellies before they stung you again, or me or Trudy. And it worked. They're gone."

"Do you have any idea what you've done? You've brought yet more doom to my people. I must get the head back." She tried to stand again, with the same results.

"Well, you're welcome," Trudy said. "We saved your life. Now you owe us."

Shoal narrowed her eyes. "I know."

"That's right, and we intend to collect." She stared down at Shoal like a judge passing sentence. "You can start by telling us why you're so hot for the *What-Is-It??*"

"Actually, seriously, what *is* it?" I interjected.

"It is the head of the witch Skalla," Shoal said.

"And she is no bauble to be gawked at. Your uncle is lucky she didn't curse him and his museum into a hole in the ground, to be eaten by worms all the screaming days of his endless torment. And yours too."

"Ah!" I said, unreasonably satisfied. "So it *is* an important head."

"Yes. And I must retrieve it." Another attempt to stand, and her knees wobbled. She fell back down.

"Take it easy," I said. "You should probably see a doctor."

"I have no time for your doctors. I must get Skalla back from the jelly creatures. If I don't, my people will be doomed always to be flotsam."

"There's that word again."

Trudy got out her pen and notebook. "You might as well tell us. You're in no condition to go chasing after jellyfish right now."

Shoal gritted her little teeth. She knew Trudy was right, and she hated it.

"And Thatcher did just save your life," Trudy prodded further.

On the other hand, Shoal had also saved *my* life when she took the sting intended for me. "Shoal, we want you to tell us what's going on," I said. "But we won't force you."

Trudy shot me an annoyed look, but I wasn't going to back down. I didn't want to take unfair advantage of Shoal, even if she was a thief. I figured we owed each other.

Shoal swallowed.

"I am Shoal, daughter of Coriolis the Last, king of a people once proud. Our home was an island-city, a rich place of beauty and music and science. But the witch—the head in the box—cast a curse on us, and the city fell beneath the waves, all its treasures and wonders and beauty—all drowned. The witch's curse was not just on the buildings but also on us, the people. Now we live most of our lives at sea, drifting in the currents, rolling with the storms in the Drowning Sleep. Then, at summer's start, on First Day, we land with the waves on Los Huesos beach. We serve the boardwalk. We work the booths and the rides. We draw the tattoos. We grill the sausages and sell the T-shirts and are enslaved until Last Day arrives at the end of summer, when the sun tires and the air begins to chill. Then we turn away from the tourist shops and midway games. We abandon the roller coaster. We leave half-completed tattoos on our customers' arms. We trudge across the broad beach and walk into the waves, and the water fills our lungs as we drown once more. We have no choice in this. We are Flotsam."

Trudy scribbled away like a newspaper reporter.

"Whoa," I said, as gently as I could, because it's

never a good idea to poke crazy people. "It kind of sounds like you're saying you're from Atlantis."

Shoal thrust her chin out defiantly. "That *is* what I'm saying."

That made Trudy snap her notebook shut and tuck her pen behind her ear. "You're talking nonsense. Atlantis is a myth. And it was supposed to have been located all the way on the other side of the world. Even if there actually was an Atlantis, it sunk thousands of years ago. How old are you? Twelve?"

"I tell you, I am the princess Shoal, daughter of King Coriolis, monarch-in-exile of the lost city-state of the last Atlantis. There have been many Atlantises. When the original sunk, we scattered to all corners of the globe and built new cities. Ours was the last one, hidden from the outside world by magic to foil your compasses and satellites. And now even that is gone. We Flotsam are the last of our kind."

Trudy blew air skeptically out her nostrils, but she opened her notebook again. "Okay. But what *really* happened to your Atlantis? I'm not buying this curse story. Was it an earthquake or a tsunami or something like that? Or was it the result of your scientists delving into arcane areas of knowledge that man was not meant to know?"

"I'll bet you a dollar it was the arcane-areas-of-knowledge thing," I said.

"I will tell you this only once more: it *was* a curse, cast by the witch Skalla. Her body was lost, but her head still lives, and we must take it back from the jellies before she can do more harm." She paused and seemed, of all things, embarrassed. She went on in a softer voice. "I ask for your assistance. Help me recover the witch, and I will answer all your questions."

Trudy checked with me, and I nodded.

"It's a deal," I said.

Shoal forced herself to her feet, Trudy holding her by the elbow, either to make sure she didn't fall or to prevent her from escaping.

I wasn't crazy about the idea of facing the jellyfish boys again, but what else could I do? Go back to my little bed closet in Griswald's museum and spend my entire summer dusting the exhibits and feeding the cat while Trudy and Shoal faced dangers and mysteries and adventures?

"What are we waiting for?" I said.

But apparently I was the only one waiting.

Trudy and Shoal were already crawling out the hatch.

CHAPTER 6

Trying to keep up with Trudy and Shoal, I watched out for stingrays and venomous shellfish and foot-eating eels. Meanwhile, Trudy grilled Shoal.

"Do you actually *live* in that shipwreck?"

"It is a hiding place," Shoal said, her eyes set dead ahead as she maneuvered around rocks and seaweed. "I have been staying there during the day, concealed from such creatures as the jellyfish boys. But they found me. They always do, Skalla's monsters. They are her hands, and she never stops grasping with them. Even asleep, she remains lethal and evil."

"Where do you go at night?"

But Shoal didn't have time to answer. We rounded a big rock, and the jellyfish boys were on the other side, struggling to push their bikes down the beach, their flat tires no doubt punctured on the same sharp rocks and spiny things I was hoping to avoid.

They heard us coming and turned around. I wished they hadn't. Griswald would have traded his right arm and tabby cat for the chance to display the jellies in his museum.

One of the jellies still had the *What-Is-It??* tucked under his arm.

"We will sting all of you," he called out. "Your throats will swell and close, and you will die fighting for breath, drowning in your own—Hey! *Ow!*"

The *ow* was in response to the rock I'd thrown at him. This time, I wasn't going to let them get close enough to touch us.

"Right idea," Trudy said, firing off a rock with a slingshot apparatus from her backpack.

"Yes! An excellent tactic! I shall launch projectiles as well!" Shoal joined in, and the three of us kept up a steady bombardment that made the jellies' stingers useless. Every time I heard a *thock* or a *crack* or an *owie*, I felt gratified.

We were almost too successful. The jellies turned to run, but they were taking the *What-Is-It??* with them.

I still didn't quite buy Shoal's tale of Atlantis and witches and curses, but I'd committed myself to helping her get back the head, and there was no way I was going to let the jellies get away with it. This was one of those times when I absolutely required an athletic success. I'd had one or two in my life. The most recent example I could remember had happened the previous school year on the soccer field. I was the goalie that day, and I was spectacular. Not only did the opposing team fail to score, but I made it obvious they never would. I frustrated them. I humiliated them. I made them weep in their sneakers.

Okay, so maybe it wasn't a championship game or anything like that. It was just a recess game, one of hundreds that year, nothing that would go down in the record books. Probably nobody but me even remembered it. But that one great game? I'd remember it for the rest of my life.

That's what I needed right now.

The jelly carrying the box had almost reached the water when I flung a small round stone. In my mind, it weighed as much as a bowling ball. I nailed him right on the wrist, that bony part that bulges out, and I heard the sound of impact: pain. He yowled and dropped the box in the gravel, and that's when Trudy got him in the back of the head.

That was enough for both of them. They splashed into the surf and swam for it until they were finally beyond the range of our whizzing rocks. Their heads ducked under the water and didn't reemerge, and our rocks kerplunked in the ocean.

"Are they drowning?" I asked.

"Their kind don't drown," answered Shoal, dropping the last rock in her hand. "They are not people. They are not fish. They are both." She ran up to the fallen *What-Is-It??*

Trudy and I traded grins. We'd driven off our enemies! And we hadn't gotten hurt in the process! This was even better than my day as an awesome goalie.

Then Shoal had to go and spoil my mood.

"The box is open!"

Trudy and I hurried over to her. In the tussle, the box's lid had come unlatched, revealing the head inside. The face was chalky white flesh. Long gray hair, stiff as wood, fanned out in spikes. The nose was shriveled and narrow, like a fish's fin. Its eyes were sealed behind puckered, sand-caked eyelids. I realized I was looking at a real human head, and I was sorry I'd ever laid eyes on it. Yet I couldn't look away.

"Quickly, we must muffle her!" Shoal said.

Trudy started rooting around in her backpack. "I've got some duct tape in here . . ."

But we were too late. The witch's eyelids popped open, revealing frosted white irises. She blinked twice, and then her eyes focused on me.

She began to speak.

Trudy rushed forward with a strip of tape to cover the witch's mouth, but the witch laughed, and Trudy froze midstride. The laugh started as a good old-fashioned witch's cackle. Then it rose higher, like a shrieking wind, like shattering glass, like splintering bones. It was a sound of insanity and cruel magic, and when the laugh fell away, the gulls stopped crying. The waves stilled. The beach became so quiet I could hear the *click clack* of crabs scuttling over rocks.

Her awful milky white eyes turned toward me.

"Why, hello, young man. And who are you?" Her voice was like slugs covered in rust.

"Don't tell her," Shoal warned, but she didn't need to. I'd read stories about witches and evil magicians, and I knew giving your name to these types gave them power over you.

"Do you think I need something as worthless as your name to net you?" the witch croaked. "The sea doesn't know your name. The sea doesn't care. Yet she can still shatter your body against the rocks. She can drive you down into the drowning depths. Did the water-princess tell you what happened to her people? Did she tell you the price I made them pay for their arrogance and treachery?"

Trudy stood poised with the tape, Shoal beside her, but neither of them moved forward. It was as though the witch had frozen them. Maybe with magic. Maybe just with fear. Either was enough to pin me in place, but Shoal had said we needed to keep the witch from talking, so I decided to do what I did best: fill the air with my chatter.

I spoke in a big rush, not giving her a chance to interrupt.

"Shoal told us everything. She told us that you weren't always just a volleyball with eyes and a mouth. You used to have a body with legs and arms and knees and that little dangly thing that hangs at the back of your throat, what's it called, oh, yeah, a uvula, and maybe you don't have one now and that's why your voice screeches like an old chicken."

"Thatcher, don't—," Shoal said.

But I was on a roll now. Talking felt like running downhill at full speed. I couldn't stop. I didn't want to. I was talking. It was the thing I was best at.

"It must be really weird, just being a head in a box, everyone looking down on you, leaving their cola cans on your face, not even bothering to use a coaster. It's too bad you're just a witch, because I bet there're a lot of other things you could do for a living. I'm thinking head of cabbage, or soccer ball, or we could drill three holes in your skull and bowl strikes with your head."

"Thatcher!"

This time I caught the alarm in Shoal's voice. It was too late. My motor was running, and I didn't even know what I was saying anymore. Just words, filling the air, and it didn't feel right anymore. I was just blabbing to drown everything out with verbal machine gun fire, and I couldn't stop.

Until I followed Shoal's gaze and saw how she looked down at the witch in wet-eyed terror.

Only then did I shut up.

Skalla's lips were moving, and her voice came from all around us in a storm-wind howl. Sea spray blasted us. Heart-shuddering thunder cracked over the sea. The ground shook beneath our feet, sending loose rocks and sand tumbling down the cliffs. The witch's withered lips parted to form a smile as a wave crashed, blanketing the beach in sizzling foam.

I couldn't tell what, but I knew for absolute certain something had changed.

"There now, my guppies. There now. It has been a while since I've done what I just did to you."

"What just happened?" Trudy demanded.

The witch let out a happy sigh. "You and the boy proved yourselves to be the princess's friends. How touching. How warm. So I have rewarded your friendship. You three will share everything now. Your lives. Your fates."

"No, you did not," Shoal said, miserably. "You did not! I hardly know them. They are not really my friends! You *did not!*"

"Of course I did. I hope you see now that it is useless to fight me. I know too many words. Too many secrets. And I have friends here, much worse than my jellies. Yes. I will rest now. But we will talk later, my guppies. I have no doubt. Yes, we will, my three little Flotsam."

With that, the witch closed her eyes. She sighed an exhausted sigh and fell silent.

CHAPTER 7

I didn't feel cursed. More like itchy and twitchy from all the weirdness and fear and excitement. And guilty.

"Uh, hey, listen," I said with the waves booming behind me. "I shouldn't have popped off at the witch like that. It's just, you know, I'm verbal. That's what the school counselor says: 'Thatcher must learn to quell his overabundant verbal energy.' She means I talk too much. I do it whenever I'm angry. Or nervous. Or bored. Or sometimes it's just because my mouth is moving and it sort of takes on a life all its own and—"

"Thatcher?" Trudy said.

"I'm still talking?"

"Yes."

"I'm sorry. And not just for talking right now."

"I'm beyond furious," she said, each syllable like the sharp blow of a hammer. Then she took a breath, and the taut lines of her face softened a little. "Being sorry doesn't get us anywhere. But I know you were trying to help. What we need to do now is head back to the boardwalk and sell cotton candy."

"Cotton candy?"

"It doesn't have to be cotton candy. It could be taffy. People want taffy, and I will provide it. I will be Trudy the taffy girl."

Shoal, who'd been busy affixing tape over the sleeping witch's mouth, sealed the box and latched it. "It's the curse. It's taking hold of her. It will take you too. You will be a slave to worthless souvenirs and non-nourishing foods and carnival games. At the end of summer, when my family drags themselves across the cold sand and walks into the waves to sink, to drown, to drift, you will be with us. You are like us now. You are Flotsam."

"What? Don't be ridiculous," Trudy said with a laugh. "I'm fine. Maybe a little stretchy. Stretchy and pully. Taffy makes you happy, *get your happy taffy!*"

I grabbed her by her arms and screamed in her face. "Trudy! Get ahold of yourself! It's the curse.

You don't really want to sell taffy. Think! You're a detective! And a superhero! And . . . and you want to run the ring-toss game. Toss a ring, everyone's a winner, everyone gets a prize!"

Oh, no.

The curse had its hooks in me too.

I could feel myself pulled in the direction of the boardwalk, as if the midway were a giant magnet and I were made of iron filings. A tunnel was closing down over my mind, and I just wanted to stand behind the counter of the ring-toss game and take money from tourists and give them rings to toss and bark out the mindless ring-toss chant all day long. *Everyone's a winner. Everyone gets a prize.*

"No!" Trudy and I both said at the same time.

"Fight it," she said.

We locked eyes. Okay. If she could hold out, then so could I. At least for a little while.

I picked up the box and took a few marching steps toward the surf when Shoal grabbed my wrist.

"What are you doing?"

"I'm tossing this thing into the sea. Hopefully the fish will gobble it up and this will all be over and I can go back to my uncle's to pack my things and catch the next bus to Phoenix and sit outside on the front porch for a few months until my parents get home and Trudy can use her detective powers to find stray dogs and you can . . . do whatever it is you do."

"No," Shoal said. "Give her to me. We still need her."

"What for?" Trudy asked as I reluctantly handed the witch-box to Shoal.

Shoal gazed out over the water, her mouth drawn in a grim line. "The witch's magic is already in effect. It is like a disease. You two are infected, as am I and all my family. You may have resisted the first tugs of the curse for now, but the magic is still working its way through you. It will get worse."

"But aren't you also cursed?" I asked. "You go back to sea and float on the waves at the end of summer?"

"The Drowning Sleep, yes."

"Then how is it you're not stuck on the board-walk, selling T-shirts or whatever?"

"Because," Shoal said, "I have been inoculated."

"Great, then let's get Trudy and me inoculated too."

"It is . . . not that simple."

"Yeah. I didn't think it'd be," I said. You don't suffer a spell cast by a witch who's capable of destroying an entire city and then go get a shot from a nurse.

"But I will try," Shoal said. "I require a container of some kind, one that can be filled with water and then tightly sealed."

"I have such a device. I call it my water bottle."

Trudy produced one from her backpack.

"It will suffice."

We watched as Shoal warily crept up to the surf and filled the bottle with seawater.

"What do you think of her?" I asked, too low for Shoal to hear.

"I'm not sure. I still have a lot of questions. All we know for certain is that she's a thief."

"Maybe. But we don't know what Griswald was doing with Skalla's head in the first place. Lots of questions, not enough answers. If there's a chance she can remove the curse from us, I think we have to trust her."

"Okay. For now."

Shoal returned with the filled bottle. "We shall do this away from the beach. Once they've licked their wounds, the jellies will return. And they are not the worst of Skalla's minions. We must find temporary refuge. Somewhere with privacy. A place where they will be reluctant to show their faces."

"How about the taffy shop?" Trudy said. And then, realizing what she'd said, "Oh, crud."

Shoal wanted a place off the boardwalk and beach, and Trudy reasoned we needed food—rock fights burn a lot of calories, and Shoal in particular looked pale and shaky—so we trooped over to a mostly empty pancake house called Pantastic's. We settled into a corner booth and ordered breakfast. Trudy asked for protein cakes, I got a mountainous construction of pancakes and whipped cream and strawberries, and Shoal ordered smoked salmon and clam juice. It was an odd breakfast. For one thing, we were eating with a head at our feet, the *What-Is-It??* crammed into Trudy's backpack along with her crime-fighting gear. But the pancake house was a good place for this kind of meeting. The piped-in music covered our voices, and once the surly waitress delivered our food, she hid on the other side of the restaurant so she wouldn't have to get us anything else.

I glopped syrup and butter around on my plate. "What's the deal with the witch now? Is she napping?"

"Casting the Flotsam spell over you and Trudy cost her, so she must rest," Shoal said. "She wouldn't have expended so much of herself if she didn't see you as a threat. She thinks you are my friends."

"We're not," I snapped, and instantly felt sorry. I knew I should apologize, but before I could, Shoal continued.

"It does not matter if we are friends or not. Skalla

thinks we're friends. And that makes you her ene-mies, which is why she was willing to spend power to keep you from thwarting her plans. She must sleep awhile to regain her magical strength, but I do not know how long."

"But with her mouth taped up, what more can she do?" Trudy asked.

"Some of her spells are already in place, brewing in the sea and gaining potency. I do not know what their purpose is, but it is very bad. And do not presume a strip of sticky fabric can stop her for long. She lost her body and still managed to sink our city. She may just be a severed head, but she is the most powerful sev-ered head my people have ever faced."

Trudy carved her pancakes into geometrically perfect squares. "It looks like we've got our work cut out for us. First we'll have to stretch the taffy until it achieves optimum pliability and—"

Oh, no, not again. "Trudy, you're losing it," I said. "Try to stay on topic. The key is placing the bottles so close together that the ring bounces off, which makes it hard for the mark ever to win the big teddy bear and I'm talking about ring toss again, aren't I?"

Trudy confirmed it with a grim nod.

"I am sufficiently refreshed," Shoal said, putting down her fork. "It is time to perform some magic of my own. Come with me."

We found privacy behind a closed-down seafood restaurant that still smelled like fish.

"This is good," Shoal declared. "Skalla's creatures do not like places where fish is eaten."

That made sense to me. If there was a place called Suburban Boy Burgers, I don't think I'd choose to hang out there much.

Shoal asked Trudy if she had something sharp, like a pin. Trudy had sewing needles, thumbtacks, safety pins, a hat pin, an "I ♥ Los Huesos" pin, and those pins with the little plastic colored balls on the end that you stick in a map.

"Yes," Trudy said. "I have a pin."

Shoal took a few of the map pins.

"Are we going to be sticking ourselves with those?" Trudy asked.

Shoal told her we were, so Trudy dug in her backpack again and produced some alcohol swabs and Band-Aids. "Infection is a dangerous foe, as surely as any jelly creature."

Shoal swirled the bottle of seawater. Little plankton particles danced like glitter in a snow globe.

"We are all made of the ocean," she said. "We began as fish who learned to crawl onto land, who learned to breathe air and eventually became us. And the ocean remains inside us still. Our blood is seawater. Our hearts govern the currents within. We are all part of the Great Soup, and the sea is the broth. After many years of trial and investigation, my father's sorcerer recovered oil from an extinct fish that contained the ingredients to combat Skalla's magic. But all we had were a few precious drops. Not enough to rid us of the curse, just enough to help one of us resist the pull of the boardwalk, for a little while. My father gave it to me and charged me with the task of locating Skalla and bringing her to our summer palace. There, perhaps she could be . . . persuaded . . . to undo her evil magic."

Summer palace? Magic fish oil? Soup? The more Shoal talked, the less I understood.

"The fish oil magic is in my blood. Now I will share it with you. I only hope it is enough to help all three of us resist the call of the boardwalk until we find a more permanent solution."

Using Trudy's pin, she pricked her finger and let three drops of blood fall into the water. Spidery threads dissolved and turned the water pink.

"We're not supposed to drink that, are we?" This summer had been unpleasant enough without me having to go vampire. But that's not what Shoal had in mind. She handed the bottle to Trudy, and Trudy pricked her finger with a deft jab of another pin and bled into the water.

It was my turn. I swabbed my finger and the pin, and then before giving myself too much time to think about it, stuck myself.

It hurt worse than I expected, and I thought Shoal and Trudy should know that, so as I bled into the water bottle, I described to them in precise detail how much it hurt. I have a good vocabulary, and at one point Trudy actually took down a few notes.

In truth, it wasn't the pain that kept my lips flapping. I was trying to cover up something else, a strange feeling that, by mingling my blood with theirs, I had bound myself even more to these two girls whom I hardly knew.

When I had a Band-Aid over my throbbing fingertip, Shoal took the bottle and shook it around, mixing the rose-colored water.

"Sea and blood," she said, "the soup of life." And then she whispered some other things that weren't in English. It sounded nothing like "hocus pocus" or "abracadabra," but it did sound like magic, and as she continued to speak, the water lost its pink color. Within moments, it just looked like plain seawater again. Shoal dumped the water out.

"There," she said, giving the empty bottle back to Trudy. "It is done."

And I did feel a little different, a little more like myself. The need to stand around hollering, "Everyone gets a prize!" was still there, but not as urgent.

"How about you, Trudy? Still obsessed with taffy?"

But Trudy didn't respond.

I looked over toward her. Or, rather, toward where she'd been standing.

She wasn't there anymore.

There was just her hand, desperately clutching, as she disappeared down the storm drain.

The steel bars that should have prevented anything larger than a milk carton from falling into the drain were bent back like pipe cleaners. Looking down into the concrete-lined channel, I spotted one of Trudy's sneakers lying in the muck like a dead animal. I scooted through the gap in the curb and dropped with a splash into muddy water. Shoal followed.

I picked up her shoe and we took off at a run through the stinky darkness. Twigs and leaves and fast-food wrappers and cigarette butts and pulpy rotted I-don't-know-what washed over our feet and ankles. The channel ended several blocks away at the beach, where the filthy water flowed past more bent steel bars and down a trough into the ocean.

I leaped through the remains of the grate with Shoal beside me and charged down the beach. At the surf line, Trudy was locked in combat with a fish. Or a fish-thing. Hunched over, it must have been at least fifteen feet tall, marching into the water on muscular green legs. A long dorsal fin ran down its spine, all the way to the end of its dragging tail. It held Trudy's backpack in one arm. In the other, it held Trudy. She kicked and beat at it with her fists, but the fish didn't even seem to notice.

Sprinting toward the water, I launched myself at the monster fish and caught it by the tail in a running tackle. The fish didn't care. Sharp spines on its tail scratched my flesh. Breakers crashed over my head. I wouldn't let go. But with a flick of its tail, I went tumbling, landing on my back in the shallower water. The fish turned to look at me. Its eyes were black and mindless. A mustache of tentacles as thick as baseball bats trailed in the water. It opened its gigantic mouth in a great gawp, then turned away and continued on, unperturbed.

"Hold on, Trudy!" I screamed, coughing saltwater.

Shoal darted by me in a flash. She took off like a cannonball and landed on the fish-thing's back, then proceeded to smack its head with a length of driftwood.

I had never seen anybody fight so viciously. Not even in the movies. Not even in a video game. Blood seeped from under the fish's scales, and its lips parted in a silent scream, its tentacles kicking up water as they thrashed in agonized fury.

Shoal's assault worked. The monster dropped both Trudy and the backpack and retreated toward the safety of deeper waters.

"To shore!" Shoal called, scooping up the backpack and hugging it to her chest while I helped drag Trudy onto land.

On the beach, with our wet hair glued to our heads, we all looked like sodden rag mops. But we were alive, and we'd kept Skalla's head out of enemy hands. The only sounds were our panting breaths and the strangely calm lapping waves.

"Come on," I said. "Let's get some distance from the—"

Shoal's legs went out from under her, long tentacles wrapped around her ankles and dragging her across the sand. Several yards offshore, the fish stared at us with its dumb, glassy eyes.

Trudy and I each grabbed one of Shoal's arms, her hands still gripping the backpack.

"Let it go!" I screamed, my heels dragging across sand and rocks as the fish pulled her backward.

"No! It wants the head!"

"It'll take you *and* the head!"

Trudy released her hold of Shoal, but only to take a folding knife from her pocket and slash away at the tentacles. The fish moaned in a hornlike baritone but kept pulling Shoal away.

We were losing her. I dug into her wrists with my fingers, fearing her arms would pop from their sockets. But my grip gave first, and Shoal slid away. In a last, desperate effort, I dove to the ground, hoping to grab Shoal by her hair, her ears, her throat—anything to keep her away from the gawping fish. Landing face-first, I reached out, my nails scraping her arms. Two more tentacles whipped out and attached themselves to the back of her head.

"Take it," Shoal said, shockingly calm. She tossed me the backpack. I caught it on reflex. Then, "Seek my father!" she called. "Neptune House! The summer palace! After midnight! IIe cannot help you before then! The curse . . . I am still alive! I am still—"

And she was still saying that when the fish lifted her into the air and deposited her in its bathtub mouth. It closed its rubbery lips, and Shoal was gone.

The fish sank below the surface.

Waves gently rolled ashore.

I ran back into the water, feeling beneath the

foam and gravel with my hands, looking across the waves for any sign of her. Every moment she was gone stretched into a new forever. I scanned the shoreline up and down, searching. When enough time had passed, I realized I wasn't looking for a fish or a drowning girl.

I was looking for a body.

CHAPTER 8

We need to notify the authorities," Trudy said, getting her phone out.

"You don't think it's too late?"

"The last thing Shoal said was she was still alive. If that fish was one of Skalla's creatures—and considering it was the size of all three of us put together and walked on two legs and, ack, tentacles, then I'm pretty sure it *was* one of the witch's pets—I don't think it wants her drowned. It wants her alive. For . . . I don't know what. So I'm going to assume we can still help Shoal."

That made sense. I got out my own phone and punched numbers.

"Emergency 911 operator, state your emergency," said a bored voice on the other end.

"A fish ate my friend!" I bellowed.

"Louie, I told you not to call here when you're drunk." There was a click, and the line went dead.

I immediately hit redial.

"Emergency 911 operator," the same voice said with a tired sigh. "State your emergency."

"I'm not drunk! My friend got eaten by a fish!"

"That can happen when incompatible fish share an aquarium. It's not an emergency."

"My friend isn't a fish, she's a girl, and a fish ate her and we need help, like boats and ships and divers and helicopters!"

"You said a girl," the operator said. "You mean a girl fish? A female fish? Still not an emergency."

"She's not a fish!"

Trudy placed a call of her own, to federal authorities up the coast in San Francisco.

"Operator, please listen carefully," she said. "We are reporting an emergency. In the interest of getting the most appropriate assistance dispatched immediately, I will relay the situation as accurately as I can: a gigantic, amphibious fish with arms and legs has swallowed our friend. We need a full-scale rescue effort involving the fire department, the coast guard, and the navy, and we need it *now*."

A pause, and then she hung up.

"What'd they say?"

"Fffzzzt mwah mwah fffzzzt," Trudy reported.

We needed a landline, or somewhere with a better phone signal. Trudy said her place was nearby, so we made an exhausted sprint to her mom's bookstore.

The shop occupied the corner of a low-slung brick building on Main Street. Unlike the other shops around it, the bricks were scrubbed clean and the sidewalk out in front swept and tidy. Used books with crisp, bright covers were displayed in the window. The place looked pleasant and sunny. It totally didn't fit in Los Huesos.

"Hi, Mom, this is my friend Thatcher we're going to hang out upstairs don't bother about lunch see you later!" Trudy said even before the little bell on the front door stopped jiggling. I caught a blurry glimpse of a surprised woman in a sweater polishing the cash register, and then Trudy was dragging me upstairs to the apartment where she and her mom lived.

It was tiny compared to my house in Phoenix, but after a couple weeks of sharing tight quarters with Griswald, Sinbad, and the shrunken heads, it was nice to be somewhere that felt like a home. The overstuffed sofa and chairs looked worn but comfy, and none of the knickknacks gave me the heebie-jeebies.

Trudy dialed 911 on the landline, but things went the same way they had on the beach—just distorted fuzz. We weren't surprised.

"The phone company always says it's because the salt in the air eats through the cables," Trudy said, putting the receiver back in its cradle. "But I bet it's the witch's influence. On to Plan B, then."

"Which is?"

"Shoal told us to find her father."

"Right. She said something about Neptune House. And the summer palace. Any idea what she was talking about?"

"Maybe there's something in one of the books downstairs—"

"Trudles!" Trudy's mom appeared at the top of the landing. "That's no way to introduce me to your new friend."

I liked her right away. She reminded me of my kindergarten teacher, with a pair of glasses hanging around her neck on a string. Within seconds she'd swept me over to the kitchen table, sat me down, put a Coke and a plate of oatmeal cookies in front of me to give my stomach something to do while she made us lunch, and cheerfully assaulted me with questions. Did I like living in Los Huesos? What did my parents do for a living? Was I a fan of squirt guns? What was it like to spend my summer in a museum? Did I know what I wanted to do with my life? Is there a God, and if so, what is His or Her or Its plan for humanity?

"Mom, I'm going to show Thatcher the store while you finish fixing lunch."

"Oh, splendid. Are you an avid reader, Thatcher?"

"Yes, he is, very avid," Trudy said, hauling me downstairs.

"She's friendly," I said once we were among shelves crammed tight with hundreds of books. "It's nice of her to make lunch."

"She's thrilled I'm hanging out with a real-live human being, even if it's just you. I haven't made any friends since we moved. Mom feels guilty about it."

Trudy was a little unusual, maybe, but not so bad that she shouldn't be able to make friends.

"Your folks are divorced?" We'd only known each other a day, but since we'd been through so much, I felt comfortable asking rude questions.

Trudy didn't seem to mind. "Yeah. Long time ago. Dad's a regional sales manager for a plumbing fixture company. Toilet parts."

Interesting. I'd been sure her dad would be a cop or an FBI agent or a nosy reporter.

"So, what made you decide to become a superhero-detective?"

She started rooting through a cardboard box full of books on the floor. "I live in a town with hardly any kids and where most of the adults I encounter are cursed carnies from Atlantis. You think I should be playing with Barbies?"

"Put it that way, and I guess being a superhero-detective makes a lot of sense. Does your mom know about all the crazy stuff that goes on here?"

"I tried to tell her once, but remember, until today, I didn't know much myself. Just that there were weird occurrences and strange people. Anyway, with her bookstore dream, Mom's in her own little world."

I thought about my own parents, and how focused they were on their squirt guns, and I understood.

Trudy began sorting through another box. She picked up a skinny little hardcover book and flipped through pages of black-and-white photos. "What about you? What was your life like before you came to Los Huesos and got cursed?"

I tried to imagine what I'd been up to in Phoenix before summer. And what I'd be doing if I'd stayed home. Probably hanging out at the mall and the water park and the miniature golf course and complaining about being bored.

"Right now," I said, "I am having the most memorable time of my life."

"Aha! Look!" Trudy handed me the book.

On a crackly, yellowing page was a grainy black-and-white photo of something I could only describe as a palace—a three-story castle made of coral, with concrete waves curling against the walls. Figures of mermaids and giant squid and sharks and a great sailing vessel decorated the entrance. The photo caption said "Neptune House," which, according to the book, had been a ballroom back in the 1920s, the centerpiece of the Seven Seas Gardens amusement park.

I read on. "It says here it got hit by a bad storm in 1924 and had to be condemned. The rides and stuff on the boardwalk were built afterward, to replace the original amusement park. Then the old park ruins caught fire a few years later, and the Seven Seas site became a gathering place for the 'destitute and criminal.' "

"Sounds promising, doesn't it?" Trudy said.

"Yeah. But Shoal said the Flotsam wouldn't be back at their palace until midnight. It's easy enough for me to sneak out from Griswald's—he's not what I'd call a very guardy guardian—but what about your mom?"

"Maybe the old pillows-under-the-sheets trick and a recording of me snoring . . ."

"That really works?"

"Sure, especially if I devise a pneumatic bellows system of some kind to simulate breathing . . ."

"How about we tell her you're staying over at the museum?" I interrupted before she could make plans to construct a complete Trudy robot. Not that I didn't believe she could do it, but we were a little pinched for time. "You did say she's happy you made a friend, even if it's just me."

"She'd want to meet Griswald first, to make sure he's okay."

"That's a problem. He's not okay. Far from it. If he was keeping Skalla's head in his care, then he's probably loyal to her."

"But if that's true," Trudy said, "it's not safe for you to go back. You could become a shrunken head with fish fins for ears, or worse."

"Yeah. Well. Someone's got to feed Sinbad."

"You said the cat's fat, so I think it'll be all right. Thatcher, I'm serious, you could be right about Griswald. It's too risky—"

Griswald chose that moment to come hobbling down the sidewalk, right past the shop window. He was looking down, muttering something to himself, and didn't see me and Trudy watching him go by.

"We should follow him," I said. "If he's a bad guy, we might catch him in the act."

"In the act of what?"

"Something evil. Or at least nasty."

Trudy nodded in agreement. She called upstairs: "Mom, can we have our sandwiches to go? Thatcher has to . . . um . . ."

"I have to go dust something stinky," I helpfully provided.

Trudy's mom came down a moment later with a pair of brown paper bags. She enthusiastically informed us that they were stuffed with apples, carrot sticks, and tuna fish sandwiches. The thought of eating fish made my stomach wiggly, but I thanked her as Trudy rushed us toward the door.

Poking our heads out, we watched Griswald cross the street and duck into a squat building down the block.

We made our way over in an awkward combination of speed and nonchalance. A parking meter maid rode by in his little cart, gave us a stink-eyed scowl, but kept going. A few blocks away, a delivery truck rumbled away from the hardware store. Other than that, the streets were abandoned. Pretty typical for Los Huesos.

Trudy and I paused across from the building Griswald had gone into—the Shipwreck Tavern, his favorite bar. Instead of windows, there were portholes, painted over black. A faded mural facing the street depicted a sinking tall ship, complete with floating wreckage and drowning sailors, their faces frozen in terror at approaching shark fins.

"I'm going in," Trudy said, jogging across the street.

"It's a bar, Trudy. Twenty-one and up. You have a fake ID?"

"Oh. Right. Hmm. This will take some subterfuge."

We circled around behind the Shipwreck to a gravel parking lot. There were no cars, just a lonely trash Dumpster.

"Here's the plan," Trudy said. "I'll scream 'fire,' and when someone runs out the back door to see what the fuss is about, we'll knock them out and then sneak in."

"Knock them out? You have knockout spray?"

"My science teacher wouldn't give me the right chemicals, unfortunately. Okay, then, how about we use these." Out from her backpack came a small brick of firecrackers and a plastic lighter.

"Fourth of July comes early to Los Huesos, I see."

"These are leftovers from Chinese New Year, actually."

"Let me guess: we light them and drop 'em in the Dumpster. People come running out, and in all the confusion they don't notice us sneaking in through the back." Just in case Trudy missed the completely mocking tone in my voice, I did things with my eyebrows to indicate how dumb I thought her plan was.

Trudy missed the tone of my eyebrows.

"You got it. Hopefully there's nothing that will catch fire in the Dumpster."

"Or, we could try that," I said, pointing. At ground level was a small, dark window. Checking around to make sure no one was watching, I tugged on it. It swung forward on hinges, just an inch. I bent down and heard Griswald's distinct, gravelly baritone. It was just a rumble; I couldn't make out actual words.

"I have an idea," I whispered. "We'll need string."

"What kind? I've got fishing line, nylon rope, cotton twine, copper wire—"

"I'll take the fishing line."

I explained my scheme and, with a disappointed look on her face, Trudy put away her firecrackers and gave me a spool of line, as well as her phone. I think she really would have rather blown something up.

Flipping open her phone, I tied the end of the spool around it. Then, after setting my own phone to silent ringer, I used her phone to dial my number.

"Voilà," I said. "Instant spy device."

Holding my own phone to my ear, I lowered hers through the window, just a tiny bit at a time. If Griswald's murmuring stopped, I would assume he'd noticed her dangling phone, and we'd run away like a couple of rats on fire.

But the murmuring kept on, fuzzy and weak through the phone, until finally I could make out the words.

". . . been looking for him for hours now. All

down the boardwalk, all through the town, but he's elusive. No, he's not alone. He's found a friend, a girl from town. They were spotted with the princess at the pancake house, but by the time I got there, they'd pulled up anchor."

My stomach gave a little kick. He was talking about us.

"They're definitely sticking their noses where they don't belong. My fault for bringing the boy out here, but when his mother asked if I could watch him for the summer . . . Well, I couldn't say no. But I should have. It's critical we find them. For one thing, they've got Skalla's head."

He'd called the witch by name. He knew her. He knew what she was. And he knew we had her. My worst fears were being confirmed.

"My plan is— Hey, wait a minute. What's that?"

"He sees the phone," I whispered to Trudy.

"Pull it up! Let's get out of here!"

I almost did. But then Griswald said, "Oh, my mistake. I'd never noticed that urinal there, is all. They're normally not that shade of green. At least not originally."

I breathed a sigh of relief that they weren't talking about the phone and made a mental note to never, ever, ever use the bathroom at the Shipwreck Tavern, even in case of dire bladder emergency.

"Very well, lads," concluded Griswald. "Looks like we've got our work cut out for us."

It sounded like the meeting was breaking up. We could make our escape now, but I was tired of skulking about, and I wanted to find out what Griswald knew about Skalla and Shoal and the Flotsam.

"I'm going down there," I announced to Trudy.

"What for?"

"To face him."

"Okay," Trudy said. "I'm with you."

After pulling the phone back up through the window, we walked around to the front of the building and barged through the front door. No reason to be sneaky now. It took a while for my eyes to adjust to the dim lighting, and then I saw a bar fringed by dry palm fronds, shellacked blowfish, little glass lantern globes, and netting strung with cork floats and plastic hula girl figurines. Farther back, down some stairs and through the open men's room door, was Griswald, caught in the act of conspiring with his cohorts, who happened to be a flock of seagulls.

They looked at Trudy and me with their blank bird eyes. They pooped. That's about all they did.

"Ahoy, I found you!" bellowed Griswald triumphantly.

"More like we found you," Trudy countered. "And now we know whose side you're on."

He apparently didn't have a comeback for that. Instead, he hobbled past us, up the stairs and out the door. He began heading down the street.

"You kids aren't as clever as you think," he grumbled as we trailed him. "It's obvious to anyone who's paying attention that you're sculling along coastal waters you have no business getting near."

We followed him down past the hardware store and post office, aiming toward the beach. "You may think I'm deaf and dumb, sitting in my museum with my scrimshaw and jars of formaldehyde, but I have friends in this town. Watchful friends. Talkative friends."

"Please tell me you're not talking about the seagulls."

"Pretty handy, aren't they?" Griswald said smugly. "Nobody notices a gull unless it's trying to take off with your catch. A seagull is the best lookout a sailor could wish for." He glowered darkly at us. "And my friends told me what you've got in your backpack."

There was more talk of mutinies and stowaways, none of which seemed to have anything to do with the matter at hand, until we arrived in front of the museum. Griswald pulled on the door. "Hmm. Something's wrong with this blasted knob . . ."

"Um. Did you lock it?"

Griswald blinked, then smiled as bright as the

rising sun. "Aye, that's right. That's why I'm so glad you came out here to visit, Thatcher. Every old captain needs a crew, and you've got the makings of a good one. Both of you."

I didn't get it. One second he was all Captain Hook, and the next he was Admiral Affable.

"Anyway," he said, his face growing sober, "the witch isn't someone you want to play with. I've crossed her before. It didn't go well. It never does."

He tried the knob again, jiggling it uselessly. I couldn't stand it anymore, so I gave him my spare key.

"Good lad," he said, unlocking the door.

We went inside with him. For some reason, I wasn't afraid of Griswald anymore. I felt sorry for him. Besides, this was the guy who used to send me five-dollar bills tucked inside birthday cards with pictures of mermaids on the front. I knew he was odd. But in my heart, I couldn't believe he was evil.

Trudy got out her notebook and clicked her pen. "What did you mean when you said you've crossed the witch?"

"Fought her!" Griswald said. "Did battle, me and my friends. We're Keepers, you see, watchers of these shores. Everyplace where sea meets land has old-timers like me, pledged to keep nasties at bay. Why do you think more towns aren't eaten by sea serpents?"

Only a few days ago I would have said because

sea serpents weren't real. But now I realized it would have been a stupid thing to say, and for once I didn't say the stupid thing.

"But Skalla is different," Griswald went on. "She's older and nastier. With or without a body, she's spiteful. Jealous. Hungry for power. And when you anger her, she *punishes* you."

He swept his arm in a gesture that included all the exhibits: the Feejee Mermaid, the shrunken heads, the sea bishop, the water-goat, Little Mister Fishy Pants, and the Sea Dragon Who Wears a Hat. "Here's her legacy of evil," Griswald said. "My friends who dared to stand up to her. People once as real as you two, now transformed to these abominations."

Trudy stopped writing. She gazed around the room, her eyes passing over the glass cases and the hideous things stored within. "You're saying . . ."

Griswald nodded. "Thatcher, Trudy, meet the Keepers."

I waved at the exhibits. Nothing waved back.

"I got lucky," Griswald said. "I almost managed to outrace Skalla's voice as she was in the middle of casting a curse on me."

"Almost?" Trudy repeated.

Griswald pointed to his head, shaking his finger as if he were scrambling an egg. "She did this to me. So much of what I knew is lost, my thoughts scattered like flotsam on the sea. And it's frustrating. There are ways to beat the witch. There are artifacts in my museum that could help us, if only I could remember. So many of my memories remain beyond my reach, just over the horizon. There was a submarine death trap, I think, and a harpoon cannon."

I supposed a death-trap submarine and a harpoon cannon could be pretty traumatic.

"But *we're* here now," Trudy said. "Maybe we can help you remember." She poked at a tottering pile of boxes in the corner.

"Not so fast," I said. "How do we know we should trust him? Just because he *says* he's an enemy of Skalla's doesn't mean anything. Sometimes people lie."

"Thatcher's right," Griswald said to my surprise. "The witch changes people. Warps 'em. She even warped *me*. Here. I'll show you."

He lowered himself to a stool. "Skalla destroyed an entire city, and even that didn't sate her appetite for cruelty. She casts her curses out of anger. She casts her curses to get revenge. She casts them to get her way, and sometimes she casts them for pure, malicious amusement."

He looked down at his leg. I didn't want to see what he was about to show us, but if we were going to survive the summer, we had to know everything.

"Griswald . . . I mean, Uncle Griswald. What did Skalla do to your leg?" Another of my rude questions. It was turning out to be a rude kind of summer.

He began rolling up his pant leg. Instead of the stump I was expecting, his leg ended in something much worse.

The fish tail where his knee should have been was covered in scales as blue as the sea on a sunny day.

CHAPTER 9

Griswald turned out to possess a surprising talent for charming Trudy's mom. We all trekked over to her bookstore and within minutes he'd gotten himself invited for dinner. By the time we'd picked our way through a meal of grilled haddock and green beans, Ms. McGee was nearly insisting that Trudy spend the night over at the museum.

"What. The heck. Was that about?" I demanded of Trudy once we returned to the museum.

"What?"

"My uncle and your mom! I'm surprised she didn't send us home with pie!"

"Oh, she did," Griswald said guiltily, wiping meringue from his beard.

"I don't know," Trudy said. "But she always had

crushes on the waiters at Captain Shrimp's Seafood Shack."

"Never underestimate the influence of a good chowder," Griswald said.

At thirty minutes to midnight, we all loaded into Griswald's car and headed off for Neptune House, the Atlanteans' summer palace in the old, destroyed amusement park. Griswald drove down the two-lane road hugging the beach in his 1972 Ford LTD, a big tank of green steel that creaked and swayed on its springs with the slightest motion of the steering wheel. The ride felt like being on a boat in rough seas and, sitting in the back seat, I looked around for a life jacket. Griswald peered into the fog and muttered a sea chantey about shipwrecks and sharks.

"Do you have any tips on dealing with the king?" Trudy asked him. She still had her notebook out and had been peppering Griswald with questions, but she didn't get much out of him since his mental focus seemed to have gone out with the tide.

When we'd left the boardwalk at least a mile behind, a loud pop came from the right side of the car. I'd been in a car with a flat tire before, so I knew what it felt like. We flappety-flapped along for a few more yards, but once we hit a particularly rubbly patch of road, it was clear we weren't going to get anywhere this way.

"I hope you have a spare," I said, getting out to inspect the damage.

"Why, of course I have a spare," Griswald said with indignation. "It's the jack I'm not so sure about."

Five minutes of rooting around in the trunk turned up a lot of things—some rope, a golf scene carved into a sperm whale tooth, and something that might have once been a Twinkie—but no jack.

"Don't you worry," Griswald assured us. "When you're at sea, you make do with what you have. I remember the season I spent on the *Mad Guppy*. She was a ninety-foot trawler sailing out of Dutch Harbor and as fine a ship as you could want. So what if her hull was a bit rusty—"

"Hold on," I said. "Before you finish this inspiring anecdote, let me ask you one thing: Where's the *Mad Guppy* now?"

"Well, she's on the bottom of the Bering Sea, but that's not my point—"

"It's ten minutes to midnight," Trudy said. "We were hoping to beat the Atlanteans back to the palace. We've got to get moving."

But we wouldn't be going in the car. We'd either have to wait for a tow truck or find another way.

Trudy unfolded a map. "How far is it to walk?"

"That depends," Griswald said. "It's not the same distance every time. Depends on the tides, the moon, and the stars. And you can put that map away, missy. Nothing concerning the Atlanteans is down on any map. True things never are."

Trudy shot him a suspicious look. She still didn't trust him any more than I did. "Then how were you planning to get there?"

He didn't answer right away, chewing his gum as though he was trying to come to a decision. With his fish leg, there was no way he'd be able to hike far, and I figured he'd try to talk Trudy and me out of going on our own. But he just sighed and pointed down the road.

"Set a course that way and go until you can go no farther," he said. "I'll get this tire fixed somehow, and if you beat me to the palace, I'll at least pick you up to take you home."

Trudy cinched up her backpack, and I cinched up my pants. Cinching just seemed like the kind of thing you do before heading off into unknown territory. We set off without another word, but after a few yards I stopped and looked back at Griswald. He was leaning on his crutch and fiddling with the rope from the trunk. Only a day before I'd have been happy for any excuse to get away from him. Now, even though I still wasn't sure about him, I felt bad about leaving him behind.

"Don't you worry about me," Griswald said. "It's

been a long time since I've had allies, and allies can give even an old hardtack biscuit like me some freshness. I'll be fine. You just look after yourselves. You're each other's lifeboat. Never forget that."

We left Griswald alone in the fog.

The road beneath our feet grew more and more crumbled, and the air before us thickened into a wet wall that swallowed Trudy's flashlight beam. We passed a junkyard where a Doberman rushed the fence and growled, jolting us into a run until we figured out it was just a dog, and then we kept going, our hearts kicking in our chests. There was a welding yard, and a burned-out building that might have once been a bar, and then we left the town behind us. A lone, mournful truck horn faded in the distance, but we saw no traffic.

The road ended at a wall of tangled brush. We pushed our way through, into a field of dry scrub. In the still air, I could hear waves crashing ashore. Somewhere a seal barked.

Rusty contraptions like the remains of squashed steel spiders punctuated the field: roller-coaster tracks and whirly rides abandoned in place when the amusement park was wrecked almost a hundred years ago. I felt like we were walking through the graveyard of a lost civilization. And then I remembered that, in a sense, we were.

We kept walking until Trudy's light landed on a monster. Or at least a plaster sculpture of one. A shark the size of Griswald's car was entwined by ivy, its gaping maw a nest of windblown straw and spider webs. Even in its decrepit state, I recognized it from the book back at Trudy's.

Trudy roved her flashlight across the shadows and revealed a great, towering mass of plant growth, in which were trapped mermaid figures and a Spanish galleon. We'd come to the right place.

We waded through the weeds and found a pair of doors, thick with grime and powdery dust. "Should we knock?" Trudy asked.

"Nobody ever answers the door at a haunted house," I told her in my very best lecturing tone. "You have to slowly swing the door open, take a couple of steps inside, and then the door slams shut behind you and locks you in. Then you and your friends go your separate ways and get slaughtered one by one."

"My mom doesn't let me watch those kinds of movies. She says they'll give me nightmares."

I took hold of the doorknob. It turned with buttery smoothness, and I slowly pushed the door open. Trudy and I took a couple of steps inside.

Behind us, the door failed to slam shut with a diabolical will of its own.

Trudy shined her flashlight across the vast circular

hall. A chandelier of conch shells and pearly abalone hung from a domed ceiling sixty feet above our heads. A grand staircase swept gracefully to upper galleries. Over the windows hung beaded curtains of sea glass and coral, chiming soft music in the breeze we made with our movement. I could imagine young couples dancing to orchestra music back before color television, when everything was still black and white.

On the walls were painted strange, flat figures, sort of like you'd find in an Egyptian tomb. Trudy and I moved slowly along the curve of the wall to examine them, Trudy snapping pics with her camera while I held the flashlight.

The pictures seemed to tell a story, like an ancient comic book: a great city rose above the waves, slender towers reaching for the clouds. Below, people played musical instruments, made paintings and sculptures, pointed telescopes at the stars. The next scene showed the interior of a palace where, surrounded by piles of gold and jewels, a figure in leopard-seal robes and a seashell crown sat on a throne. I recognized the person in the painting. She was depicted in cartoony two dimensions and was younger, with her head attached to her body, but there was no mistaking the expression of evil glee on her face: it was Skalla, the witch.

In the next set of pictures, Skalla gathered more and more treasure while the people below grew thin and hollow-eyed, their ribs drawn in stark lines across their torsos. They tended kelp fields and labored in smoke-belching factories, with slave-drivers cracking whips across their backs.

But one man with a great curly beard raised a black sword above his head. Leading a wave of people hefting sickles and clubs and trident spears, he stormed Skalla's throne and cut her head off.

The eyes in Skalla's head remained wide and staring. She opened her mouth as if to speak, and the city fell apart into sharp fragments, like shards of glass. Flames and waves consumed the island, and the people floated like garbage on the open sea.

In the second to last picture, Skalla's head landed on a shore. I recognized the rock-and-driftwood beach, the shape of the cliffs. It was Los Huesos, and Skalla was surrounded by monsters: giant squid and strange hybrids of humans and sea creatures.

In the very last scene, the people of Atlantis washed up on the same beach. Skalla and her creatures were there, waiting for them.

"This is everything," Trudy whispered. "The whole history of the Flotsam, right here before our eyes. Skalla ruled as a tyrant, but the king, Shoal's dad, rose up against her and gave his people freedom."

I turned away from the wall. "And then she made

him pay. Him and everyone else. But where are they now? Let's check upstairs."

But we wouldn't be getting up to the second floor, at least not under our own power, because lining the elegant ballroom stairs, dressed in faded and worn clothes, unshaven, red eyed, glaring fiercely, were at least a dozen men and women. They all held three-bladed spears pointed at Trudy and me.

One of them stepped to the front of the group. She was tall, her eyes glinting like green sea glass in the sun. I was certain I'd seen her before. Yes—she worked at the bike and skate rental on the boardwalk. The blades of her spear were stained reddish brown. I hoped it was just rust.

"Greetings, mud walkers," she said. "Welcome to the summer palace of Coriolis, King of Atlantis Lost."

Overall, this hadn't been the friendliest of welcomes, but it could have been a lot worse.

Then the bike lady said, "Prepare to suffer."

That was more like it.

CHAPTER 10

At a gesture from the bike lady, the Flotsam rushed us and threw us to the floor. I kicked and flailed as a man pressed his elbow into the back of my neck, grinding my head into the hardwood slats. He yanked my arms behind me so hard I thought every tendon from shoulder to wrist would snap. Through the corner of one blurry eye, I could see Trudy getting the same treatment. Griswald had warned us we might not get a warm welcome, but he hadn't said the Atlanteans would attempt to kill us on sight.

I tried to tell them we were friends of Shoal, but with my lips mashed against the floor, my words came out as garble.

"Utter not a sound, mud villain," the bike lady said. "You do not face vendors of candies and amusements now. At this moment, we are the Atlantean royal guard, and whether our home be a paradise or a hovel, we shall protect it. Give us a reason, and you will see what becomes of our enemies."

I had a feeling whatever she was threatening might involve filleting. Possibly battering and deep-frying too.

Our attackers yanked us to our feet, the jagged tips of their spears hovering inches before our eyes.

"The girl," Bike Lady said. "Take her bag."

One of the Atlanteans produced a long serrated knife that looked like the kind of thing whalers would use to remove blubber. He held it against one of the straps of Trudy's backpack.

"You don't want to do that," I said.

The spear points were suddenly even closer to my eyes.

The man with the knife paused, checking with Bike Lady to see if he should go ahead and saw through the strap, and maybe through Trudy's arm.

Bike Lady stepped up to face me, her eyes as hard and sharp as coral chips. "Speak, mud boy."

Trudy sighed. The last time I'd conversed with a strange and dangerous person, I'd gotten the Flotsam curse cast on us.

"Okay, see, it's like this: Skalla's head is inside the backpack and supposedly she's sleeping because I ticked her off and she responded by using magic against us and I guess it tired her out. But that was hours ago, so maybe she's waking up. There's tape over her mouth to make sure she doesn't say anything but it's not like tape's a magic substance that never gets unsticky, especially in the damp and salty air and—"

"Silence!"

I bit my tongue. Hard.

Bike Lady looked really upset, as if she'd just lost control of things and didn't know what to do next. She motioned at the knife guy to step away from Trudy. Her clenched jaw bulged so much, I was sure she'd be spitting out broken teeth. They'd be sharp fragments and would probably go through my heart.

Thinking about it, I should have mentioned right from the start that we were friends of Shoal.

"Can I just say one more thing?"

"No," Trudy and Bike Lady both said at the same time.

"Take them to . . ." Bike Lady paused, unsure. I figured the next word would be "dungeon." Or "torture chamber." Instead, she said "kitchen."

Since kitchens were places with more knives, not to mention boiling pots of oil, I was in no way relieved.

They frog-marched us into a cluttered room of dirty tile floor and walls that might have once been black-and-white checkerboard. Battered pots and pans and cleavers hung from hooks. The cleavers bothered me. At a stove, a stoop-shouldered old man in chef whites (or almost-whites) stirred a dented cauldron of soup. He took no notice of me or Trudy or the Flotsam until Bike Lady cleared her throat.

"Fin?"

"Busy. Cooking."

"Fin, we caught these intruders—"

"Busy. Cooking. Soup." He continued stirring.

Exasperated, Bike Lady tried again: "Fin, these children . . . they are *with the witch*."

"Hmm. Come here and taste this."

"Fin—"

"Soup! Dinner! Taste it!"

Bike Lady's hands balled into fists, but she went forward and took a slurp. "Cabbage soup, yes, very nice. As I was saying—"

"Yes, cabbage soup. I suppose you are disappointed it's not polar kraken," the cook said. "Perhaps if somebody had caught a polar kraken, I would prepare polar kraken for His Royal Highness. Alas, His Exalted Majesty's hunters were only able to spear three heads of cabbage, so that is what you will be served at His Extreme Grace's table. Speaking of whom, where is our king?"

"Leading a search party to find the princess," she answered, her face turning red in frustration. "And as these intruders have brought with them our most terrible enemy, I have no doubt they know the princess's fate."

"We do," Trudy said, straining against the two Flotsam clutching her arms. "Shoal was swallowed by a monster fish. We're her friends, and we've been trying to help her."

At that, the Flotsam gasped. Except for Fin.

He offered his spoon. "Would you like some soup?"

"No, I would not like some soup! If you're not going to help us help Shoal, then let us go!" Trudy was steamed, and in a roomful of angry Flotsam with trident spears and racks hanging with ugly cleavers, I didn't think anger was a good idea. Not that I could blame her, but I wanted to make sure we didn't end up as key ingredients in Fin's pot.

"Sir," I said, faking a reasonable tone, "we are Shoal's friends, and she told us to come here because she said you were her family. We have the witch's head with us, and she put the Flotsam curse on us. Whatever mess we're in, we're all in it together."

Fin took another taste of his soup and made a sour face. "It's not even good cabbage. Concha, tell your guards to let the children go."

"But Fin—"

"Do it."

Concha, the bike lady, gave a reluctant nod, and her guards released us. All the moving parts in my arms creaked and popped as I stretched them, trying to restore circulation.

"Now," Fin said, "I would like to have a look at the thing in your bag. Will you permit me?"

Trudy nodded. She removed her backpack and very carefully set it down on the kitchen counter. Concha and her guards held their breaths, spears ready, looking more scared than angry as Fin gently pinched the zipper and opened the backpack, just enough to peer inside.

"Well, by Poseidon's eye socket, that's her all right."

He rezipped the backpack and motioned for us to join him sitting a long kitchen table. Spread across the scarred wooden surface was a big sheet of butcher paper covered in dark ink markings: lines, curves, circles that might have been planets, and scribbles lined up like math problems. Fin dipped a pen in a small, squid-shaped pot of oily black ink and scratched out some notations.

"What is all this?" Trudy asked, examining it with her nose a bare inch off the table.

"This represents what has become my life's work, done in service to my king: attempting to calculate Last Day, when the curse calls us back into the Drowning Sleep. It is dependent upon a convergence of high tide and deep ocean currents and planetary alignments. Every year I get closer to figuring it all out, but then Last Day arrives before I can solve it and we're called back to sea, and no matter how cleverly I think I have hidden my chart, one of Skalla's minions steals it while we're adrift. Every summer I must begin anew, from scratch."

"I don't understand why the curse works like this," Trudy said, annoyed at her own lack of understanding. "If Skalla hates you so much, why not just drown you outright? Why keep you coming back here every summer?"

"Ah, because she needs us, you see. We don't know what for, but she has a plan for us, so the very same spell that condemns us also keeps us alive. The currents bring us to this beach that, in old days, was Skalla's hideaway, her refuge and stronghold. We wash ashore here every summer, and the witch keeps us enslaved to the tourists, humiliated."

"But not after midnight," I pointed out. "Here, right now, you're not all zombified."

Fin steepled his fingers. "We are a strong people. Even as our hands squirt mustard on hot dogs, we fight. Years ago, with the help of our few land-dwelling allies, we almost won a victory. As the king's sorcerer, I used my own small magic, and we gained this modicum of freedom—a place of our own to dwell in the longest hours of night, where we can plan, and calculate. Even if it is all for nothing in the end."

These land-dwelling allies Fin mentioned—he was talking about the Keepers. Like my uncle.

"So when is Last Day?" Trudy asked.

Fin smoothed out the butcher paper. "There is an unusually strong high tide due soon, the strongest of the century. It coincides with the full moon, an arctic storm, the approach of an undiscovered comet, the venting of an underwater volcano, the braiding of geomagical force lines. . . . It is very complicated. But I believe I know when."

"And 'when' is . . . ?"

"Three weeks from today."

Trudy and I exchanged wide-eyed stares.

"Three weeks?" I shouted. "We've only got three weeks before we're all floating garbage?"

"Oh, it is even worse than that," Fin said. "Something even larger is happening this year. More than merely Flotsam being drawn to the drowning. I have been unable to put my finger on it, but I believe there is a disaster coming. I do not know its nature, nor its magnitude, but who is to say it won't be of a proportion even greater than the storms that befell the last Atlantis?" He paused. "Are you sure you wouldn't care for some soup?"

Another Flotsam entered the kitchen. I thought I'd

seen him selling churros on the boardwalk. "The king has returned," he announced. "He demands the witch and prisoners be brought before him."

"They're not prisoners," Fin said. "They are guests and allies."

"Perhaps you would like to tell the king that," the newcomer said.

Fin thought about it. "You had better go up to have your audience," he said to us in a conspiratorial whisper. "It won't be so bad. If he puts you in the dungeon, I will bring you soup. If he does worse . . . well, let's hold that thought in reserve for now."

The Atlanteans took Trudy and me up to a huge room on the second floor. I figured it had once been a dining hall. Fin followed us, carrying Trudy's backpack. A chair of driftwood, adorned with pearls and spiky frills of coral, loomed at one end of the room. Leaning against a seat back made from a giant clamshell, the man sitting in the chair watched without expression as Trudy and I were brought before him. He wore a T-shirt with a faded crown on it and a tan raincoat thrown over his shoulders like a cape. With one hand, he stroked a long, braided beard fastened with a gold hoop—a napkin ring. His other hand gripped a trident spear. Back on the boardwalk, he'd told me that I was smelling the scent of the sea, and that I should buy popcorn. In this setting, he seemed very different.

"I am Coriolis," he said. "Welcome to my court."

He pulled his lips back in a smile like the last thing you'd see before a shark bites your face off.

"We have sought Skalla the witch for many summers. We thought we had defeated her some years ago, in one of our many battles. I cast her off the fishing pier myself. It was not the first time. Her head rolls on the sea floor, through mud and muck, down in the trenches where the only light comes from glowing fish. This is where she learns her secrets. But she always returns here, like Flotsam in her own way. Of late her whereabouts have remained unknown to us. And now, here she is again. I would very much like to hear how you made her acquaintance. But first, I would know this: *Where is my daughter?*"

For once I did the smart thing: I let Trudy do the talking. She told him everything, from Shoal stealing Skalla's head, to the jellyfish boys and the monster fish, plus everything in between.

"Shoal said we should come to you," she concluded.

Coriolis didn't say anything for a long time. He didn't move. He didn't even blink. He was like a big firecracker with a long, burning fuse that you regret having lit because no matter how far you run, you know it's going to blast your fingers off.

"Sire, they are lying," Concha said. "They belong to the witch. You cannot believe Shoal would go off on her own to steal Skalla's head. If she discovered its location, she would have told you, and you could have dispatched me and my guards to retrieve it. She would not have acted alone."

"You speak as though you've never met the king's daughter," Fin said. "That is precisely the kind of thing she would do. She is impetuous, foolhardy, and brave. Not unlike her friends. And if she thought the best way to take Skalla's head was to steal her in the night, then it is a good thing she didn't tell you first, because you and your guards are as stealthy as a walrus with a distressed stomach."

Concha opened her mouth to protest, but the king held his hand up and a thick silence settled over the chamber.

"I would see the witch now."

Fin stepped forward. "Allow me, sire. I have a gentle touch." He unzipped Trudy's backpack and, as if he was handling a bomb, set the *What-Is-It??* on a side table beside the king's throne. After carefully unlatching the lid, he opened the box. The witch's eyes were still closed and the duct tape Shoal had put over her mouth still in place.

And then her eyelids moved like the wings of a moth.

"Let me kill her, sire," Concha pleaded.

"No. Ending her life could mean ending the curse. Or it could mean losing any chance of ever ending it. That is our dilemma. We have had opportunities to kill her in the past, but we cannot know the consequences. We cannot stab or smash or boil our troubles away."

Concha pounded her fist into her palm. "And what has our restraint earned us, sire? We remain enslaved, selling cotton candy to tourists. What of your daughter? If these mud walkers are telling the truth, then Skalla holds her captive in a prison fish. We must end the witch, my king. Now, while we have the opportunity."

Coriolis rose to his full height. He hadn't looked that massive beside the popcorn cart. He glared down at the *What-Is-It??* and said, "There will come a day when my hatred of this creature will surpass my sense of responsibility. I feel it coming, soon. Then, I will teach this witch the true meaning of suffering." He closed the lid. "But that day is not now."

Sounds came from downstairs: a window breaking, heavy footfalls, and screaming. Someone called out, "Get the head!"

Coriolis and Fin hurried down the stairs with a

few Flotsam guards, leaving Concha and several of her men and women to watch the head.

Trudy and I raced downstairs. Dozens of creatures swarmed the lower floor, shaped like men but with faces armored in hard, speckled brown shells. Instead of hands, they gripped clubs in giant lobster claws. An Atlantean swung his trident at one of the lobster men, who caught it in his pincers and snapped the shaft in two. They all wore I ♥ Los Huesos T-shirts.

It didn't take an expert in military history to see how the battle was going. There were only a couple dozen Atlanteans. There was a whole school of lobsters.

In the center of the skirmish, Coriolis said something in Fin's ear. Fin nodded and hurried upstairs, dodging several lobsters and bashing a few more.

Coriolis turned to Trudy and me. "It falls on you now, friends of Atlantis. The witch's servants will make more attempts to reclaim her. You must not let them. Foil her plans any way you can. More than just Atlantis rests in the balance. And . . . if you can help my daughter . . ."

"We will," I promised. And I meant it. We would.

"Then remove Skalla from here. We shall fight to cover your escape. Now go," he ordered. And he dove into the fray.

Fin came running down the stairs with Trudy's

backpack. He thrust it at Trudy, and she ducked her arms under the straps.

"Follow me!" Fin shouted, leading us back into the kitchen. He flung open the doors of a cupboard beneath the sink. "It's a quick escape from the palace. Not safe, but safer. Do not forget what the king said. It all falls to you now."

"Why don't you come with us?"

Two lobster men burst into the kitchen, pincers snapping.

Fin took a meat cleaver from the knife rack over the stove and faced the lobsters. "Obey the king!" he ordered us. "Go!"

I took a last look at Fin grappling with the lobster men and followed Trudy into the dark.

CHAPTER 11

Banging my knees and elbows and head, I rattled down a metal chute in the dark until coming out an opening and dropping through empty air. I was grateful when something cushioned my landing.

"Getoffameyoulummox!"

That was Trudy.

"Sorry," I said, rolling off her and helping her up.

Muffled sounds from the battle above echoed down the chute as Trudy moved her flashlight beam through the dark space. We were standing on the narrow concrete edge of an underground river. A strong current flowed down the channel.

"I think this is a ride," Trudy said. "Or at least it used to be."

We'd seen the ruins of roller coasters and toss-around-throw-up rides up above. This appeared to be the inevitable scary Tunnel of Love.

Trudy pointed her flashlight above our heads. "Hey, are those . . . bats?"

Trapped like flies inside sheets of cobwebs, bats the size of kites leered down at us with glow-in-the-dark eyes.

"Fake bats," I said. "But let's get out of here in case I'm wrong."

We jogged along the water's edge, and then, when the space narrowed, scraped along the wall until there wasn't even enough room for that.

"I guess we go swimming," Trudy said.

"My clothes still haven't dried from the last time we went swimming. I haven't been dry since my plane from Phoenix landed. My socks never stop squishing and my underwear chafes."

"Are you done complaining?"

"I'm not complaining actually. I'm getting used to being soaked and salty."

"That could be the result of the Flotsam curse," Trudy mused. "Some kind of psychological adjustment to the idea that we're going to spend fall and winter and spring adrift on the seas."

"Okay, actually, I *was* complaining. I'd give anything for a change of pants."

A creak of wood and sloshing of water interrupted me before I could speak longingly of warm socks and underwear from the dryer. Trudy and I braced ourselves for the next new danger in the dark.

A miniature pirate ship approached, the paint chipped but still gaudy where it remained. From a mast no higher than my head flew the skull and crossbones, carved out of wood.

"It's not a tunnel of love without a ship built for two," I said, and since the boat was heading in the same direction we were—out, hopefully—we climbed aboard.

This wasn't my first time in a spooky tunnel of love—they always had one at the Arizona State Fair—but this was my first time riding one alone with a girl. Ordinarily it would have been weird, crammed so close beside each other, wondering if we were supposed to hold hands or do other stuff. But I felt comfortable with Trudy. We were at war, and there was nobody I'd have rather had in a foxhole with me. And, come to think of it, she smelled kind of good.

Then she aimed her flashlight in my face and blew my eyeballs to smithereens.

"Hello? Blindness? Ouch?"

"Sorry," she said, redirecting the light to the tunnel walls. The tunnel was lined with murals painted in the same style as those we'd seen up in the palace.

There was a mix of scenes from Atlantis, with grand ceremonies and celebrations and heroic fishing expeditions, as well as scenes from the boardwalk. I recognized Coriolis at the popcorn stand. And I felt a pang of desire as we passed by a scene of the midway games and the ring toss, with stuffed animals hanging from racks like executed criminals.

"Who painted these?"

"The Flotsam, I bet," Trudy said. "Probably trying to preserve their history. To tell their story."

There was writing on the walls, some of it undecipherable, some in English, laid out in segments so we could read it as our boat floated by. One section read:

OF SHOAL'S MOTHER

The queen of Atlantis perished with the sinking of the island-city and thus never suffered the Drowning Sleep. Our king, however, suffered both their shares. For in autumn and winter and spring, he enjoyed no life, cursed like the rest of his people to drift in slumber. And in summer, he suffered life without his beloved. His heart was a cold stone submerged in a cold sea.

But one summer, he met a woman. Shirley, she was called. In the language of the land-dwellers, her name meant "bright meadow." She came from the land of Detroit, but seeking escape from a colorless life spent toiling in offices, she was drawn to the endless possibilities of the broad, open sea. She found a job in Los Huesos, making doughnuts in a shop near the beach. At night she fried bear claws and crullers, but in her time off she would roam the boardwalk, up and down, not minding the smell of seaweed and fish. For here, on the edge of the land, she could look out over the ocean, beyond the limits of sight. She would imagine the wonders hidden unseen in the depths, and dream of mysteries and possibilities.

One day, she met the king of Atlantis, who sold popcorn. He had never met a land-dweller who could lift him from his cursed daze, who could make him forget the smell of butter-flavored oil and remember who he was. In her own way, Shirley possessed a kind of magic. They fell in love.

At the end of summer, the king left Los Huesos, as all Flotsam must, and Shirley found herself alone, carrying a child within.

Yet the king returned the next year and rejoiced upon being greeted by Shirley and *their daughter, the new princess of Atlantis Lost.*

There were hopes for young Shoal. Since she was half land-dweller, half Atlantean, perhaps she would be spared Skalla's curse. Perhaps this one, this last daughter of Atlantis, would break the evil cycle.

But at summer's end, when the tide dragged the Flotsam back into the unforgiving waters, not even the strength of a desperate mother could keep the infant Shoal from crawling into the waves for her first drowning. Shirley swam after her, but she swam so far she could not find her way back to land. And, unlike the Flotsam, when her body next touched shore, there was no life in it.

"That's so sad," Trudy said.

No, it was more than sad. It was tragic. The entire story of Atlantis was just one terrible tragedy. We read more narratives, battles won and battles lost (mostly lost), and memorials for the dead. We floated past portrait after portrait marked with birth and death dates. The Tunnel of Love was a tomb.

The Flotsam themselves weren't the only things from Atlantis that had washed up on the beaches.

Wreckage that could only have come from the sunken city lined the channel. Fragments of pillars and columns. A headless statue of a muscular, fish-tailed sea god posed hurling a harpoon. A saddle that looked big enough to fit over the back of a killer whale. Everything was in bad shape, corroded and studded with barnacles but displayed with care on sawhorses and other makeshift platforms.

"Atlantis must have been beautiful," Trudy said.

Judging by just the sad remains around us, I had to agree.

"If you think Atlantis was something, you should see what's coming next," said someone in a deep croak.

Gurgling and splashing, a lobster man the size of a sumo wrestler rose from the water. He must have followed us down the chute, which meant he'd gotten past Fin and Coriolis and Concha and all the rest. And if that was true, what had happened to the Flotsam?

Grasping the boat with two claws, the lobster upended it, and we went spilling into the channel. Our feet hit the shallow bottom and we thrashed away, scrambling up among displays of Atlantean artifacts to get away from the lobster.

The tip of an antenna brushed the back of my neck. I grabbed a crusty goblet and chucked it behind me to hear it ricochet off hard lobster shell. Claws snapped over my head. Another claw slammed into the side of my skull. I went down, sprawled over the wreckage of Atlantis. Dizzy and barfy, I struggled to get up, slipping on ocean-weathered Atlantean coins and pottery fragments. My hand landed on a handle of some kind, and my fingers instinctively gripped it as the lobster loomed over me, reaching for my face with a pincer big enough to engulf my entire head. I raised my arm in defense and saw what the handle was attached to: a length of volcanic glass fashioned into a sword blade.

The pincer came down at my face. I swung the blade and shaved inches off the point of his claw.

With a whistling scream, the lobster man looked at his injury, eyes the size of billiard balls twitching on the ends of his eyestalks.

The hundreds of nicks in the blade's edge made it look even more deadly. What kind of warrior had wielded this weapon in the ancient past, I wondered. What battles had it seen? Maybe it had been handed down from generation to generation, soaking up blood and sacrifice. And now it had come to me. I was determined to do it proud.

"Back off," I said.

To my astonishment, the lobster man did.

"Back off *more*."

He did again.

"She'll win," the lobster man said. "The witch always does. You think you can fight her, but you're wrong. You think I *wanted* to be a lobster man? Look, just give up now. Give me her head. You'll be saving yourself a lot of trouble."

I swung the sword again, right into his damaged claw. The blade bit, and he screamed.

I raised the sword blade a little higher. "Get lost."

Cursing even worse than Griswald, he scuttled back into the channel.

I should have felt good. Triumphant. Or at least relieved at having dispatched an enemy and prevented the capture of Skalla's head. It's what Coriolis had told me to do.

Instead, the lobster's words echoed in the dark tunnels of my thoughts.

He hadn't wanted to be a lobster man.

But Skalla always got her way.

Skalla always won.

CHAPTER 12

The tunnel emptied into a salt marsh a few hundred yards off the beach. While Trudy consulted her map, trying to figure out exactly where we were and how to get back to the highway where we'd left Griswald, I kept the Atlantean sword ready and watched out for more lobster men.

We found our way back to Griswald on the side of the road. Using rope and a boat anchor, Griswald had managed to get the flat tire changed.

"There you are!" he bellowed like a ship's horn, hobbling over with his crutch as he saw us emerge from the fog. "I was worried about you!"

And after we'd told him everything that had happened at the Flotsam's palace and the Tunnel of Love, he was even more worried.

"I thought I saw a school of big lobsters go by,"

Griswald said as we loaded into his car. "They were driving pickups, with big bundles in the back. I would have followed them if I'd gotten the flat fixed in time."

I had a sinking feeling that these bundles Griswald was talking about were the Flotsam. We made Griswald drive us for a return visit to the palace, where my fears were realized. King Coriolis and Fin and Concha and all the rest were gone, leaving behind some snapped trident spears and just a few fragments of giant lobster shells.

Skalla had Shoal, and now her family as well. She'd do to them whatever awful thing she'd dreamed up in that disgusting head of hers. And considering that she was a 100 percent disgusting head, it was sure to be dreadfully awful.

"I hate those lobsters," Trudy seethed. "They're even worse than the jellies. We should get the biggest pot of water we can find and make fish stew from the whole lot of them. Make them tell us how to defeat their boss. Or else, they can boil."

I mostly agreed with Trudy. But another part of me couldn't forget the sumo lobster's words. He hadn't always been a lobster. Skalla's hate had made him what he was.

But Trudy was right about at least one thing:

Skalla's creatures were the key to rescuing the Flotsam.

"Uncle Griswald, do you know where we can find the jellies?"

He surprised me with a helpful answer. He knew, and he agreed to take me and Trudy there.

At the edge of a cliff overlooking the beach hunkered a row of small cottages. Once upon a time, maybe, they'd been charming little bungalows, perfect for a seaside vacation. But now they were weathered down to gray, chipped wood. Even the boards over the windows looked ancient. There was, however, one exception—the cottage in the middle. I wouldn't say it looked like a place where you'd spend money to stay, but the windows were intact, and a warm yellow glow came from inside. That was where I saw the jellyfish boys approach. They leaned their bikes against the cottage and went inside.

Trudy and I didn't even need to speak. We just nodded to each other and got out of the car, ignoring Griswald's warnings as we began cutting through ice plant and dune grass, up to the cottages. We knew it was a gamble, taking the witch's head closer to Skalla's enemies, but if the jellies knew how we could get Shoal back, we were willing to risk it.

From a small patch of dead grass in front of the

door, the rusty handle of a wagon poked out like a periscope. It hadn't been played with in a long time. There were also some soil-encrusted toy cars and a dusty, deflated football.

We walked up three sagging wooden steps and knocked on the door. Trudy held her flashlight like a club. My sword in hand, there was no way they'd get their stinging fingers anywhere close to us. After a moment, a woman with silvery purple hair opened the door. A choker of pearls ringed her wrinkled neck.

"I'm not interested in the newspaper," she said. "Not since they dropped *Mary Worth* from the funnies."

"We're not selling the paper," I said. "We want to talk to the boys."

"My boys? Are you friends of theirs?"

"Yes," Trudy said immediately.

The woman smiled pleasantly enough. "I'm sorry, they're not home."

The flat-out lie angered me, but I couldn't bring myself to take it out on this spindly old grandmotherly lady.

"Ma'am, we saw them walk up. Those are their bikes right there."

She didn't have much reaction to being caught out. She merely shrugged. "You're welcome to come in if you'd like to wait for them. I'm sure they'll be home soon."

It smelled like a trap, but since I was expecting it, I decided it was worth the risk. And actually, it smelled more like lemon-scented furniture polish than a trap. In contrast to the outside, the cottage's living room was clean and tidy. Large-print issues of *Reader's Digest* and a Bible rested on an oval-shaped coffee table in front of the sofa. A vase of silk flowers sat atop a boxy old television.

There was no sign of the jellies. Maybe they were hiding in the closet. Maybe they had a secret compartment to curl up in and be slimy together.

"Would you like some cookies?" the woman asked us.

I almost said no, but then I figured any time she spent in the tiny kitchen was time Trudy and I could spend snooping. "That'd be great, thanks."

She went off, and while Trudy peered at the shelf under the coffee table, I examined some framed photos on the wall. Most of them were of a pair of boys, twins, climbing a tree, playing with a red wagon, opening presents by a Christmas tree, riding bikes.

"That's my Tommy and Dicky," the woman said, returning to the living room with a plate of seashells. Not cookies shaped like seashells, but actual shells. She took one herself and bit into it. The shell wouldn't crack, so she put it back down on the plate and selected another. "Hmm, just a little stale. What was I saying? Oh, yes, my grandsons. They used to like being in pictures, before that hideous witch turned them into jellyfish. They're so camera-shy now."

"Does everyone in town know Tommy and Dicky are jellyfish?" Trudy asked.

"Why, I wouldn't know, but we've got nothing to be ashamed of in this house. Tommy and Dicky are good boys. They just fell in with a bad crowd."

"That happens to many youths in my peer group," I said numbly. "It's our violent video games."

"No toys or games till homework is done," the woman said. "That's the rule in this house. Or it used to be, when the boys still went to school. They had to drop out, I'm afraid. The witch has them so busy they couldn't keep up with their courses. Also, because they're jellyfish." She picked up the plate of shells and held it out for Trudy. Trudy took two.

"Thank you. What sorts of things does the witch have them do, if you don't mind my asking?"

I was happy Trudy could get her question out. Me, I was struck dumb by the woman's openness.

"They won't try to take Skalla's head back from you, if that's what you're thinking. Unfair to ask that of them again, I think. They're just boys, my Tommy and Dicky. No, that job went to the witch's bigger helpers. You won't be able to fight them off with sticks and stones. I'm happy for that, because your rock-throwing hurt my boys. I had to give them chewable aspirin and shrimp ice cream just to calm them down."

"Are they still working for the witch?" Trudy asked.

"Oh, I'm afraid so. Once you're hers, you stay hers. Soon everyone in this town will belong to her. This town and beyond. The time is in her favor. The planets and tides and things are all in the right place. I don't pretend to understand it all, but she has the Flotsam where she needs them. Anytime now, she'll cut them open and empty them of the magic she put in them when she cast her curse. And then the soup will be on."

That's why Skalla kept the Flotsam coming back to Los Huesos. Not just to torment and humiliate them, but to keep them handy for when she was ready to work a bigger act of magic. And now that the time was near, she'd had her lobster men kidnap them. She would drain them of magic, like Shoal had bled to share her resistance to the curse with us. Only, I had a feeling what was coming next would involve much more blood and much worse magic.

"Thank you for admitting this to us, ma'am," Trudy

said. She sounded polite, but I could tell she was as alarmed as I was. "We'd still really like to talk to Tommy and Dicky. Could you ask them to come out?"

"But I told you, they're not here. As you came in, they left out the back. Why do you think I've been so willing to have this chat with you? I just wanted to give my boys time to get away from you awful children."

Trudy and I made a quick search of the cottage, just to make sure the woman wasn't lying now, but the jellies really did appear to be gone.

"You shouldn't have done that," Trudy told her. "If you know what the witch is up to, you should be helping us stop her."

The woman's eyes grew moist. "I can't," she whispered. "That's what I've been trying to tell you. So many of us have tried to fight her. But she's too strong. Even as just a head, she's too strong. Bless your hearts, but you'll lose." She sank onto the sofa and wept quietly. "We always lose."

Only then did I notice the gills sucking air into her wrinkled neck.

🐚

The boardwalk was empty the next morning, with just a scattering of tourists complaining that the shops and stands and rides were closed. Nobody manned the tattoo parlor. The popcorn stand remained shuttered.

Trudy and I searched the entire length of the board-walk and caught no sign of the Flotsam. I wondered if we'd ever see them again. Or Shoal. When we passed the midway, Trudy gripped my arm to keep me from wandering off to the ring-toss stand, and I did the same for her when we passed the saltwater taffy shop. And when we stopped to gaze out over the water, we both felt it calling us. The ocean wanted us to wade in. The waves hungered, and I could feel myself losing the will to resist.

We kept searching.

At the north end of the boardwalk, electronic beeps and blips leaked through the weathered wooden doors of a large, canary yellow building with arches over the entrance.

"That's weird," Trudy said, stopping in front. "All the rest of the businesses are closed."

I gave the doors an experimental tug. Locked. "So's this one. They probably just leave the machines on at night."

Trudy didn't seem convinced.

We stepped away, but a muffled voice beckoned us from inside: "Secrets . . . fortunes . . . reveal all . . ."

Trudy frowned. "Tell me that's not suspicious."

"It's just a video game, I'm sure. They talk. Don't you play games?"

"Well, there's an autopsy computer simulation I downloaded from the FBI . . ."

". . . secrets . . . reveal all . . . ," said the voice.

Trudy retrieved a screwdriver from her backpack. "We have to check this out."

"You realize, of course, we're probably walking into a snare," I said as she began monkeying with the door handle.

"At this point, all of Los Huesos is a snare. But we can't afford not to investigate every lead."

Unfortunately, I agreed with her.

"There!" Trudy said as the door handle and lock broke apart into fifteen separate pieces. She pushed the door open. "Just keep your sword ready."

Dim light filtered in through skylight windows high above our heads as we treaded quietly between long rows of battered video games. Some were old enough to qualify as museum pieces. Flashing messages under glass begged us to insert quarters. I felt like I was being besieged by robot panhandlers.

More games lined the back wall: pinball machines with ringing bells, Skee-Ball, a baseball game that let you knock Ping-Pong balls into scarred outfielders.

We encountered no people. No customers, no arcade workers. Except for some roosting pigeons, we appeared to be the only living creatures here.

"Zoltan knows secrets!" an enthusiastic voice rang out. "Let Zoltan tell your fortune!"

Shoved into the corner was a cluster of glass and wood-framed cases. Inside one of them, a waist-up mannequin outfitted in a dusty black tuxedo and red turban glared at us. His hands hovered over a cloudy crystal ball.

"Zoltan will tell all you wish to know! Just ask Zoltan!"

"It's just a fortune-telling machine," I said.

"Yes, and it's talking to us in an apparently abandoned arcade," Trudy pointed out.

Zoltan smiled with a wide mouth. His lips were too red. Dust coated his glass eyes.

"Give Zoltan a quarter! Zoltan will reveal all!"

"They could stand to turn his volume down," I said. "Okay, Zoltan, what have I got in my pocket?"

"Zoltan tells all! Ask a question of Zoltan!"

"Zoltan doesn't even know I asked him a question."

"You didn't give him a quarter," Trudy observed.

"Fair enough." I dug out a quarter and shoved it into his coin slot. Whirrs and buzzing and creaking and *boing*s came from inside the wood case. Zoltan turned his head a little to the right, then left, as though stretching a stiff neck.

"Ask a question of Zoltan! Zoltan will tell you everything!"

"Where are the Flotsam?"

Zoltan's hidden speaker buzzed. Then, "Ask Zoltan a question," he said. "Zoltan will tell you all he can!"

"Zoltan's an idiot," I said to Trudy. "Come on, let's go."

We got a few steps away when the fortune-telling machine blared at us: "Zoltan can't tell you what you need to know if you don't ask Zoltan the right question!"

We turned. He looked back at us with his frozen, ever-smiling face.

Trudy approached Zoltan and stood close. She got out her pen and notebook.

"Zoltan, are you alive?"

The mannequin looked back at her, smiling with his red lips, silent. Trudy continued to stare Zoltan down. She was pretty formidable, but I figured she'd blink first since Zoltan didn't have moving eyelids.

I jumped when Zoltan blurted out, "Zoltan tells fortunes!"

Trudy took a deep breath. "Zoltan, how can we find Shoal and the other Flotsam and nullify Skalla's curse and also avert the big disaster Fin said is coming in three weeks?"

"Ask a question Zoltan can answer! It costs but a quarter!"

"Maybe I haven't asked the right question yet. Let's try him again." Trudy looked at me expectantly.

"What, you carry cameras and firecrackers and doughnuts but you don't have a quarter?"

"Thatcher . . ."

"Okay, okay, here."

I inserted my second-to-last quarter, and Zoltan's body shuddered like an unbalanced washing machine.

Trudy cleared her throat. "Let's try this: Zoltan, what *do* you know?"

And Zoltan said, "Sorrow."

The other half-dozen fortune-telling machines lit up, fizzing with static and squeaking and grinding. They all started speaking at once, their voices colliding in the morning chill. It was impossible to make out everything they were saying, but here and there I was able to pick out a few words and phrases:

". . . was a mother . . ."

". . . was a reporter . . ."

". . . was the police chief . . ."

". . . was the librarian . . ."

Thunder boomed over the sea, a great cracking blast of sound that rolled out from the water and blanketed the town, and the voices fell away. It was as though they'd been shouted down by the sky.

"We are Los Huesos," Zoltan said, his mechanical voice softer now. "We are the ones who asked questions. We are the ghosts in the machines."

"Who . . . who were you?" I asked.

"I was always Zoltan. Bob Zoltan, of Zoltan Hardware and Garden. I had a wife. I had children." His voice grew more staticky, his words spoken more slowly. "They are gone."

His life went out.

"We're getting somewhere now," Trudy said. "Give him another quarter."

I dug into my pocket to retrieve a coin and sank it in his slot. "Last one."

Zoltan's light flickered back to life and he boomed, "Zoltan will show you your fortune!"

The clouds in his crystal ball boiled slowly like a lava lamp, sharpening into an image of a dirty sea. Wreckage and debris floated in the laundry-water waves: wood and plastic, oil slicks and parts of houses, drifting like rafts past islands of accumulated junk. Roller-coaster cars bobbed like discarded coffee cups in a gutter, and I made out the sign of Pantastic's, where I'd had breakfast with Trudy and Shoal just a short time before. There were books too. And bodies. Animals and people, floating lifeless.

"Is this what Skalla's going to do?" Trudy asked in a shocked whisper.

"It is only the beginning!" Zoltan shouted. His enthusiastic bombast only made his message more horrifying. "She will leave Los Huesos wrecked! She will drown the beaches and towns up and down the coast! Houses and shops! Highways and sky-scrapers! Her reign of destruction will dwarf what she did to Atlantis!"

I thought of how many people lived on the coast of California. And what made it worse was that Skalla was going to use Shoal and the rest of the Flotsam to achieve her goals. We had to rescue them, no matter what, before it was too late.

"What can we do?" I asked.

Zoltan's box whirred and creaked weakly. His light fluttered.

"Pain and sacrifice . . . pain and sacrifice . . . pain . . . pain . . ."

I gave him a shove to get him to stop skipping.

"Pain and sacrifice," he said, softly now, more fuzz than voice. "Pain and sacrifice. What will be your fortune?"

And his light went off for good.

CHAPTER 13

Trudy's mom stopped by to see the museum, and after Griswald gave her a complimentary tour of all the weird things in jars, she agreed to let Trudy spend another night. She left behind a tuna casserole. We ate cheese spray on old pizza instead.

Griswald had said the museum contained secrets and artifacts that might help us defeat Skalla, but in his damaged state, he couldn't remember what or where, so we spent the day searching through the exhibits, hoping to jar Griswald's memory into dredging up something useful.

"What about this?" Trudy said, holding up a tiny model ship in a bottle.

"Oh, I remember that," Griswald said brightly. "That's the SS *McPrineas*. A stolid whaler, she was."

Trudy blew dust off the bottle. "Whatever happened to her?"

Griswald squinted. "What do you mean? That's the SS *McPrineas*."

"Yes, and I'm asking—"

"He means you're holding the SS *McPrineas* in your hands," I said. "The witch shrunk the boat and stuck it in the bottle. Am I right, Uncle Griswald?"

"Aye," said Griswald. "Now she can go after only the very tiniest whales."

Trudy very carefully put the bottle back on the shelf.

The rest of the afternoon continued this way: we'd hold up an object for Griswald and we'd get nothing useful out of it. By late that night, we'd put our hands on every exhibit in the cluttered museum and still had nothing to show for it.

Time was running out, and hope along with it.

Turning in for the night (or what was left of it), I lay staring at the ceiling. All I could think about were lobster men and severed heads, and Shoal in the belly of the fish, alone. That, and the image from Zoltan's crystal ball of the wrecked Los Huesos, floating in the sea. The sight of the bodies would never leave me.

I made a decision.

When I heard Trudy snoring in her sleeping bag, tucked in the room next to mine where Griswald kept his string collection, I lowered myself from my hammock. Pulling the Atlantean sword of black glass from where I'd stowed it under my laundry, I examined the ragged edge. The blade had seen action in its days, and it was about to see some more. But I'd need a way to carry it in public that wouldn't attract attention. Remembering a movie I'd seen on television about sword-wielding immortals from Scotland who liked to behead one another, I got an idea. From the bottom of my suitcase, I dug out my raincoat (I'm an overpacker) and fetched a roll of duct tape. Then I found a poster tube in the gift shop of the museum and squished it flat to fashion a scabbard. Finally, after experimenting with placement, I taped the scabbard down on the inside lining of the coat. When I tried the coat on, having the sword up against my spine forced me to stand ramrod straight, but anyone not familiar with my usual slouch would just assume I had excellent posture.

Okay, I had my weapon. Now I needed some bait.

Tiptoeing into the hallway, I looked down at Trudy, sealed up in the sleeping bag, one strap of her backpack looped around her hand. I didn't know her well enough to know if she was a light sleeper, but in other ways, I knew her better than I did my own parents. I wished I could include her in what I was about to do. Having her with me would make me feel braver. But she'd never let me get away with it.

In Griswald's storage closet I found an old duffel with a strap similar to those on Trudy's backpack. I slipped the strap beneath her hand. Her fingers twitched. I waited. I counted to twenty, each slow beat accompanied by Trudy's sniffly inhalations. Then, with a smooth motion, I slid her backpack away. She made a noise. Murmured. Gave a little kick. And then her fingers closed fully on the old duffel strap.

Moving as quickly and quietly as I could, I stepped away from her, trying not to jostle the witch's head as I carried Trudy's backpack away.

My shoes clomped against the fog-slicked planks as I paced the boardwalk. Only the barest hint of sunlight tinged the sky in the east. To the west, the waves still came in and out like the breath of a giant.

For the fourth time this morning, I passed Coriolis's shuttered popcorn stand. It was still too early for any of the boardwalk businesses to be open, but even hours from now, the Flotsam wouldn't be back. Like Shoal, they were likely being held captive in some bizarre prison of Skalla's making.

I whistled and hummed, deliberately trying to

be noisy. Trudy's backpack swung carelessly from my hand. I could hear the *What-Is-It??* shifting around inside.

Reaching the bait and tackle shop on the south end of the boardwalk, I turned around to start another lap. Just a few dozen yards away in the gray mist stood four hulking figures.

Trouble.

Just what I'd been looking for.

Skalla's creatures would tell me where the Flotsam were being held, and if they didn't want to cooperate, they'd just see what I was willing to do to their boss.

Swallowing, I drew the sword, and they began approaching. The boardwalk was empty. Just me, these thugs, and a lone, gray seagull that gave up looking for stray bits of food among the planks and flew off.

The thugs came toward me in slow, menacing strides.

They looked like salads.

Yes, salads. Big ones. These men were made of kelp. They loomed over me as they drew close, rubbery, braided ropes and bumpy, serrated leaves draped over their bodies in cloaks of green, yellow, and brown. Polypy dreadlocks hung over faces with flesh the color of squash that's been in the crisper too long. A halo of sand fleas danced around their heads.

"Give us Skalla," one of the kelp guys said. His vocal cords sounded like mushy cucumbers. His eyes were as green as limes.

"Tell me where the Atlanteans are," I answered back. "All of them, including Shoal."

The kelp guy looked at his buddies. "Maybe he doesn't speak English." The others shrugged their green shoulders. He looked back at me. Very slowly and loudly, he said, "Give us the head. Or we'll pummel you. Pummeling means hitting."

"I know what pummeling means. I'm very verbal." I aimed the point of my sword at the backpack. "Do you know what shish kebab means?"

"Hurting Skalla won't solve your problems, mud trudger," said the lead kelp guy. "Her plans are already in motion. She's cast her curses and organized her servants. The soup's already been made. Now it's just a matter of time till it's ready to serve. So you might as well hand her over before you make things worse for yourself."

He cracked his knuckles. It sounded like snapping carrot sticks.

"Maybe," I said. "But at least the world will be minus one disgusting severed head."

"I'm warning you—," he began.

I thrust, just an inch. The tip of my sword punctured the nylon and went into the bag. The thought of impaling Skalla's face struck me as a very pleasant thought. She had it coming.

The kelp guys stepped forward, but I held my ground.

"I'm not kidding. I will perforate her. Where are the Atlanteans?"

The kelps waited for word from their leader. Ropes and leaves shifted as their muscles flexed in agitation.

"Okay, okay, we'll take you to the Flotsam," the kelp-in-chief said.

"Right, and I'll go along with you because I'm just that stupid. No. You'll *tell* me where they are." I slid the sword another inch into the backpack, splintering wood. "Now."

The lead kelp held out his hands. Long strands of green sea grass hung from his fingers. "Stop it, you little creep. I'll tell you. Just don't—don't stab the head. I—"

A sound interrupted him. A sound that chilled my stomach.

"Thaaaaatcher? Thaaa-AAAAA-aaaatcher?"

Trudy.

Her voice rang out in that little singsong people use when they're searching for someone.

"Girlfriend?" asked the chief kelp.

"I don't know her. Take me to the Atlanteans."

"I thought you said you didn't want us to take you to them."

"I changed my mind. People with swords at the heads of kelp guys' bosses get to change their minds." I didn't want Trudy anywhere near the kelps. I remembered how close the jellyfish boys had come to killing Shoal, and the kelps seemed just as dangerous. Getting them to lead me off, even if it meant heading into a trap, looked like my best bet for putting distance between them and Trudy.

But it was too late. Trudy emerged from the fog. Taking in the scene, her nose crinkled with anger. I knew she'd hate me for running off by myself, especially with the *What-Is-It??* And that was why I'd done it without telling her.

"I see you've made some new friends," she said.

The kelp men chose that moment to spring. Moving faster than a giant vegetable man should, one of them grabbed Trudy by the midsection and lifted her off the ground. The three others rushed me. I showed them no mercy. My sword whispered through the air. With an iceberg-lettuce crunch, the blade sliced all the way through a grasping arm. But my victim didn't care about his arm. He merely kicked it aside as though it were any piece of junk. Cut the limb off a plant, and it'll eventually grow back. Unperturbed, the kelp drove his fist into my jaw. It felt like getting hit by a rock wrapped in spinach. The blow drove me back, which actually turned out to be a good thing because it gave me a little space. I managed to turn the point of the sword back to Trudy's backpack, still in my other hand.

Trudy thrashed in her captor's embrace.

"Let her go or I'll chop the witch up," I snarled, my head ringing and my jaw thundering with pain. I took another step back and awkwardly unzipped the backpack. I removed the *What-Is-It??* The sword had already chipped an ugly scar in the box.

The chief kelp held up his hand to stop the others from assaulting me again.

"We're not going to let your friend go," he said. "And you're not going to kill Skalla. I know this because if you did, you'd have nothing left to bargain with. And then we'd crush your girlfriend, right before we smeared you to mammal paste."

I'd pushed things too far, and now I could see only one way out of it.

Grunting with effort, I hurled the *What-Is-It??* over the rail. It sailed in a graceful arc before dropping into the water with a deep *kerplunk*. Where it went after that, I didn't care.

CHAPTER 14

The kelps paused for a moment, stuck in indecision. Would they go after the *What-Is-It???* Or would they beat Trudy and me into messy residue?

They chose to follow their boss. Vaulting over the rail, they plummeted off the boardwalk and into the sea. I watched them surface-dive, and when I was satisfied they were 100 percent occupied with recovering the box, I turned to Trudy to take my punishment.

". . . of all the thimble-brained, dunce-headed, Thatcheristic maneuvers . . ."

I let her yell. Trudy was smart. She'd figure it out. Eventually, her tirade sputtered to a stop.

"But . . . Skalla's head wasn't in the box, was it?"

"No. I left it back at the museum. The only thing

I tossed into the drink was the box and a cannonball from Griswald's collection to make it sink. It'll take the kelp dudes a while before they find it."

"And once they do and figure out the box is empty?"

"Then they'll come at us in full force," I said. "Maybe with Skalla's entire zoo of creatures as backup. So let's get back to the museum and secure the head before they do."

I returned Trudy's backpack to her. She scowled at the hole I'd made with my sword.

"You shouldn't have done this without me," she said. "I could have helped you. I could have watched you from a hiding place, or rigged my bag with explosives, or . . . I don't know. You shouldn't have done it without me."

We didn't talk as we hurried through veils of drizzle back to the museum. I knew she was right. And I knew I should apologize. But, despite the fact that I could talk paint off a wall, I couldn't quite find the words to tell her I was sorry. Maybe because the time for sorries was long past. I hadn't brought the witch's curse to Los Huesos, but I'd brought it on Trudy, and so far I hadn't managed to do a single thing to make it better.

Anxious to escape worsening weather, we dove into the museum just as a crack of thunder shook the building to its foundations. Rain clattered against the roof like a million bullets.

"Where'd you stash the witch?" Trudy said, wiping a sleeve across her face.

"In a pillowcase under my dirty laundry. I figured the smell of my socks would keep people away."

"Good thinking."

Sinbad yowled in irritation as I shooed him off the pile of my stinky, unwashed clothes. To my relief, I found the lump of Skalla's head where I'd left it, but knowing the ruse I'd pulled with the cannonball-filled *What-Is-It??* box, Trudy insisted we look inside the pillowcase to be sure Skalla's head really was inside. It was. The duct tape still covered her mouth, but her eyelids were twitching, and the sound of her dry lips struggling to move sounded like a cockroach scuttling over sandpaper.

Back in the exhibit room, Sinbad poked his head out from behind one of the sawhorses holding up the mummy. I said his name, but he wouldn't come over.

"He seems spooked," Trudy said.

"Maybe he's just hungry. Griswald must be so busy drinking beer with the seagulls, he couldn't be bothered to feed him." I turned to the kitchen to get Sinbad a can of minced fish guts when I heard a clatter, and the sound of big things falling over, and a muffled scream.

I was starting to get used to sounds like these. It's like working in a bell factory. After a while, you barely notice all the ringing.

Another series of sharp thumps and a gruff cry, and Griswald's bulk crashed through the wall in an explosion of plaster and wood. He lay on the floor in a cloud of dust, blinking at the ceiling. His hand gripped a long brass tube studded with little switches and buttons. Affixed to it was a lethal-looking harpoon tied to a coil of rope.

"Monsters in the tunnels," Griswald said with a cough. "Help me up."

We managed to get him up on his one foot. Using his harpoon contraption in place of a crutch, he started thanking me and seemed in danger of trailing off on a story about tuna fishing near the Great Barrier Reef, so I cut him off.

"Now would be a good time to tell us about the monsters in the tunnels, Uncle Griswald."

Trudy snapped a picture of the Griswald-shaped hole in the wall. "Start with the tunnels," she said.

"Are you kidding? Start with the monsters!"

It turned out Griswald didn't have to. The monsters had followed him. A school of puffer fish on legs swarmed through the hole in the wall, and I almost laughed; they looked ridiculous, no bigger than birthday balloons, with bulging eyes and puckered fish lips. Their tails wiggled as they ran around us like excited dogs. But then one inflated to full size, expanding to a huge globe of lethal spikes, six feet across. It shoved me against a wall and mowed over Trudy.

"Stand clear!" Griswald shouted, swinging the harpoon gun around. But in the cramped quarters of the museum, he couldn't get off a shot and only managed to knock things over. Meanwhile, Trudy battled with six or seven little puffers to hold on to the pillowcase containing Skalla's head. I swung my sword at them like a golf club and sent little fish flying. But they didn't stay little. They blew themselves up like hot-air balloons. Display cases went crashing, glass exploding. A fish rolled over me, knocking my wind out and leaving me with dozens of little holes.

Woozy, I lifted myself up on my elbows, only to see the puffers deflate back to their soccer-ball-sized form and jump through the gap in the wall. One of them dragged the pillowcase along with it.

"Get them!" I screamed, and the three of us charged after them through the wall.

A bare bulb cast lemon-colored light down a narrow set of sandstone stairs diving a long way down. The bottom of the steps opened to a cavern bigger than my school's cafeteria. Crates were stacked against the walls. I read a few of the stenciled labels: *Miscellaneous Teeth. Random Severed Tentacles. Green*

Things with Spines That Smell Like Oyster Juice, Some of Which Have Tongues.

I saw no sign of the puffers. If they stayed deflated, they could be hiding anywhere.

"What is this place?" Trudy asked, her flashlight beam roaming.

"Shanghai tunnels," said Griswald. "Los Huesos is honeycombed with them. Before the boardwalk, there used to be nothing but saloons above, and not the nice kind where they clean the urinals once a week. Customers would belly up to the bar and the barkeeper would pull a lever that opened a trap door to the tunnels down here. Next thing the poor sap knew, he'd be forced to crew a schooner to Shanghai."

Treading lightly across the cave, I caught sight of a crate labeled *Strange Secrets from Deep Sea Trenches Best Left Buried*. From cargo nets overhead were suspended bundles of spiral narwhal tusks, and a giant nautilus shell the size of a minivan with portholes and a mangled propeller.

"What *is* all this stuff?"

"Hmm? Oh, you mean the collection?"

"Why, yes, Uncle Griswald, I do mean the collection."

"The beach regurgitates a lot, Thatcher. There's no room for it all upstairs, so we Keepers use the tunnels for storage."

I was glad I'd never had to dust down here.

I pointed at the shell with the propeller. "That's a submarine," I said.

"Oh, aye, she's called the *Other Nautilus*. And a fine vessel she is. She's not seaworthy, but for a death trap, aye, a very fine vessel."

Padding down the tunnel, we continued to search for the puffers, pulling crates aside and pushing barrels out of the way. Every time I nudged a coil of rope or kicked away a canvas tarp, I expected a ball of puffer spikes to leap at my face. What I didn't expect, though, was the fully inflated puffer fish that thundered by on fat, spiky legs. I managed to jump back into the wall just in the nick of time, so instead of impaling me on its spikes, it only gouged a few more shallow holes in my flesh.

"That one's got the head!" shouted Trudy.

Griswald aimed the harpoon cannon. He appeared to have a clear shot. Unfortunately, it was a clear shot at my head, so I yanked the gun out of his hands before I became Thatcher, the Amazing Boy with the Harpoon Through His Skull.

"Come on, you two! It's getting away!" Trudy's flashlight pushed against the darkness as we gave chase, leaving hobbled Griswald behind. The sound of surf echoed through the chamber, and a moment later we heard a great splash. We rounded a bend in the tunnel and came to a cave opening, just in time to see a swollen globe of spikes go under the water.

"Too late," Trudy said, along with some curse words she must have picked up from Griswald.

"No," I said. "Not this time."

I hefted the harpoon gun to my shoulder. There wasn't any point in aiming because I didn't know how to aim a harpoon gun, so I just turned it in the general direction of the puffer fish. I squeezed the trigger and the harpoon shot out with a great kick. The rope unspooled until it hit its target and then went taut.

Trudy saw what was happening before I did. Even with the harpoon in its hide, the puffer was still swimming strong.

"Thatcher, let go of the cannon!"

"Um?"

Holding the gun in a death grip, I was yanked off my feet and dragged across the tunnel floor. Sandstone crumbled as I dug in with my heels, trying to slow myself, but it was no use.

"Thatcher! Let go, you idio—" And that was the last thing I heard before knifing into the water. I was not going to let go, even as the puffer towed me out to open sea. Skalla's head was responsible for every nasty thing that had happened to me and my friends.

My finger found a switch on the harpoon gun that reeled the rope in, drawing me closer to the puffer.

I held on, into the dim murk, with pressure stabbing my ears, my lungs begging for air. My mind clouded with darkness, cold, and pain. And then there was a greater darkness, a tunnel of black rushing toward the puffer. Maybe this was Skalla's dark magic, or maybe this was Death. Maybe there was no difference between the two.

The darkness surrounded me and overtook me and closed in on me. Also, there were a lot of bubbles that smelled like fish farts.

I found myself lying facedown on a bed of slime. It stank, of course, as slime has a tendency to do. But this particular stink was familiar. It was the smell of weird monster fish. My fingers fumbled with the switches built into the gun until a flashlight attached to the barrel cast a cone of light. I was in another tunnel of some kind, pink and red and wet. Little fish skeletons and crab shells littered the ground, and ahead of me, the puffer fish lay on its side, gawping sadly. It drew in its knees and sucked its thumb, the pillowcase containing Skalla's head forgotten at its side.

A bigger fish had swallowed us both. A *much* bigger fish. Bigger on the inside than on the outside. I could stand inside it. I could even breathe inside it.

I forced myself to my feet. The walls and floor and ceiling undulated with nausea-inducing motion.

Keeping the harpoon gun level, I grabbed the pillowcase, then backed away. "Gotcha!" To keep my hands free, I tied the ends of the pillowcase around my belt, letting the head dangle around my knees.

"Thatcher?"

A voice, so faint I wasn't sure I'd actually heard it.

"Hello?" I called back.

Nothing.

Probably just my imagination.

"Thatcher? Is that you?"

I knew that voice.

"Shoal!"

Drawing my sword, I took off at a run, heading deeper into the fish.

I didn't know anything about fish anatomy, but I was pretty sure this wasn't what the inside of a fish was supposed to look like. A fish like this could only be the product of Skalla's magic. Breathing through my mouth and trying not to touch the walls, I passed through shiny, wet corridors, stepping around other things the fish had swallowed: a motorcycle helmet, a boat anchor, truck tires and safety cones, a toilet, and gelatinous blobs of undigested leftovers. But no sign of Shoal.

"Hey there, Thatcher."

I pointed my light and saw my own reflection staring back at me in the glistening meat of the fish-wall.

It wasn't alone. There were dozens of funhouse-mirror versions of me, round and squat, or stretched long and thin like a piece of chewing gum, or ruffled like a potato chip.

"C'mon, nothing to say?" said one of my reflections. "Fish got your tongue?"

"Is that supposed to be a joke?" I said. "You should have said '*Catfish* got your tongue.' See, *that's* funny."

"Not very," said my reflections. "Tell you what, Thatcher. Why don't you put down the sack and leave Skalla in here? Then we'll spit you back out. Promise."

"Thanks, but I think I can find my own way out."

My reflections laughed. It was my laugh exactly, just multiplied. "You have no idea where we are, Thatch. This fish—me, us—isn't just any old jellyfish boy or lobster man. This is one of Skalla's oldest creatures. One of her strangest. We're so bizarre and magical that we're hardly even a fish anymore. We're a pure reflection of strange things. Like you. You've come to a very bad place. Surrender her head, and we'll let you out. What do you say?"

I raised the sword. "Maybe I'll just let this do the talking."

"You'd have to chop for a very, very long time, Thatch. And time is something you've run out of."

"A guy can chop a lot in three weeks."

The reflections snorted. "Three weeks? Did the

king's sorcerer tell you that? Fin's a math weakling. You don't have three weeks. The planets are in alignment *now*. The currents have already converged. And Skalla is rested. Three weeks? Thatcher, you don't have three *hours*."

I thrust the sword down into the slime floor. It was like trying to puncture a bicycle inner tube with your thumb.

"Aw, come on, you know it can't be that easy. This is a bouncy, rubbery kind of fish-gut fun-house labyrinth. If you could just cut your way out, everyone would do it."

"Let's just see." With a sweeping arc of the sword, I sliced into the meat mirrors, right across the middle of the reflections. The blade didn't exactly cut the fish gut. Instead, things got rearranged, and my mirror-selves blurred into one another, forming a single, distorted reflection. A mouth wider than a banana sneered back at me. It was ugly, and it looked like me.

"Did that make you feel better?" the *me* said. "You're still trapped in here."

"I'm ignoring you."

"You can't ignore me. I'm inside you. You're inside me. I *am* you. Everything you do, all your weaknesses, your fears, your hopes, your desires, your secrets, your disgusting habits, your really lame jokes . . ."

"Why are you even bothering?" I said. "If you're really all that deep inside my head, then you know I only care about one thing right now. I'm getting Shoal out of here."

"Right, because you're all about helping your friends. Like you helped Shoal by chasing her in the first place when she 'stole' the box that didn't belong to you anyway. And like you helped Trudy by mouthing off to the witch and getting the curse cast on her. And like you helped the Flotsam by doing . . . well, nothing."

I opened my mouth to say something back, but no words came to me.

"You think it's bad now," the reflection continued, "but it's about to get so much worse."

The reflection kept talking. I knew what it wanted. It wanted me to talk back, to defend myself, and while I was doing that, the clock would tick even closer to disaster.

I hated every word it said because every word was true.

Well, okay. If it wanted to tell me the truth, then maybe I could get it to tell me the *whole* truth.

"I'm not so worried," I said. "I've been threatened, smacked around, cursed to be Flotsam, and swallowed by a fish. I'm cold and wet, and I've been cold and wet practically since I arrived in Los Huesos. So go ahead and tell me what's going to happen next. Or don't. Makes no difference to me."

"Nice little performance, Thatcher. But not clever enough to get me to tell you anything I don't already want to tell you."

I shrugged. "Okay then." And I turned my back to walk away.

I knew myself. I couldn't resist gloating, and neither could my reflection. I didn't even get two steps away before my reflection called me back.

"Thatcher!"

I stopped but didn't turn around.

"I might as well tell you what Skalla's got brewing," my reflection said. "It's not like you can do anything to prevent it. There's a reason why Skalla's creatures didn't just kill you outright. It's not because you and your friends are so brave or capable. It's because she needs you alive. When Skalla works a spell or casts a curse, some of her own magic, her own thoughts and the residue of her intent, is left inside the creature she worked her magic upon."

"You know I know that," I said. "It's like after Shoal extracted the fish oil that gave her resistance to the boardwalk. The magic was in her blood, so she could share it with me and Trudy."

"Well, yeah. But don't act like you understand,

because you don't. Not fully. She's going to get her magic out of you and Trudy and Shoal, too, right out of your veins. All of it. Everything's ready. Her time is here. Her magic is bubbling. She'll raise winds, and she'll raise waves, and she'll raise storms, and she'll drown the entire town of Los Huesos. Then her new Atlantis can emerge, the one her creatures have been building for her in secret. A new Atlantis she'll rule as queen of the very last island-city. So, what do you have to say about that?"

I had nothing to say.

"That's right," my reflection said. "You're out of words, and since words are the only things you've *ever* had, I guess that means you've got nothing. So why don't you just have yourself a seat and digest for a while."

I coughed. The smell of inside-fish was starting to overwhelm me. My reflection-self's words bounced around my head, as if my skull was lined with mirrors.

"It's all true," I said. "Everything you're saying about me. . . . Yeah, it's true. All true." A faint voice drifted through the fish. It was calling my name. "But what you don't get is that it doesn't *matter*. I'm doing something. I'm saving my friend. So you just glisten and talk your fishy brains out, Mirror-Thatcher. As for me, I'm busy."

Leaving my reflected image alone to sputter to

itself, I went deeper into the fish. I kept my eyes straight ahead, ignoring all the digestive burbles that started to sound like my name, spoken inside my head. Turning down another twist in the gut corridor, I found Shoal sitting cross-legged on the ground, her clothes and hair slicked with fish-belly slime. She looked lost, staring at nothing in particular. I wondered what reflections she'd seen in here. What had spoken to her?

I said her name, and she looked up.

She blinked. "It ate you too?"

"I came in voluntarily. Almost."

"Why would you do *that*?"

"Can we talk about this later? I'd like to go now."

"There is no way out," Shoal said, her shoulders hunched. "I have tried. I tried to crawl out its throat, but its lips would not part for me. I tried to pass through the digestive tract, but this fish is not arranged like other fish. I am pleased that you wanted to rescue me. That was very brave. But I fear you have doomed yourself."

"I've got something you didn't have," I said, proudly raising the mighty blade of volcanic glass. "An ancient sword of Atlantis."

She rose to her feet. "Oh, Thatcher. That is not a sword. It is an implement used for the gardening of kelp."

Oh.

Well.

Whatever.

It was still sharp.

This wasn't a time for cleverness, or talking, or even thinking. This was a time for chopping. I chopped at the fish wall. I whaled. I slammed and I sliced, again and again, until my arms and shoulders and spine ached, and then I kept chopping.

I wasn't making a scratch.

No time to get discouraged. More chopping.

So I chopped again, and when I knew for absolute certain that I couldn't swing the sword—I mean, the kelp implement—even once more, I kept on chopping.

The blade still wouldn't penetrate the inner fish wall, but something started happening. The slime floor beneath our feet wriggled. There was a rumbling. The stench of fish gas nearly knocked me unconscious. The walls and ceiling quivered, then began closing in on us.

"It's collapsing!" I shouted.

"No," Shoal said. "I believe it is regurgitating."

A flood of the foulest-smelling fluid I had yet encountered during a summer of foul-smelling fluids slammed into us. It was hot and it burned, and I pressed my eyes and lips tightly shut as I tumbled in its flow.

We passed through the fish's lips out into the sea, but we weren't much better off. Lost in a cloud of fish puke, I couldn't see anything and had no way to tell which way was up. I wondered if this was what the Drowning Sleep would feel like. Maybe this *was* the Drowning Sleep.

A hand grasped mine. It was small, but the grip was strong: Shoal. She pulled me along, my flutter kick probably not helping much, and a moment later we emerged on the surface of the waves, coughing and gagging.

"Are you still alive?" Shoal asked.

"I'm miserable, so I must be."

Still knotted to my belt, the pillowcase with Skalla's head inside bobbed on the surface like a grisly buoy.

The witch began to chuckle.

CHAPTER 15

Her laugh started as a low chortle, like someone waking up from an amusing dream. I'd heard Skalla laugh before, louder and more shrieky, but this was worse. This time, I knew she was on the verge of winning.

Overhead, the clouds spun faster, and the blue eye of the storm shrunk to a pinhole. Rain shot down, punching thousands of little splashes in the water.

"Good evening, my darling guppies," the witch said from inside the pillowcase. "Thank you for keeping me safe and cozy all this time. You're about to see what all this fuss has been about."

"Just toss her!" Shoal hollered over the wailing wind. "Be rid of her!"

"But then we won't be able to stop her!"

"We are unable stop her *now*. Perhaps we will get lucky and sharks will devour her."

"Oh, sharks are nothing to fear," scoffed Skalla. "Voracious eating machines with hundreds of teeth like knife blades? What's so bad about that?" Shark fins sliced to the surface of the water and began circling us. My heart shriveled in dread as a great bulk passed near, brushing my pants with sandpaper skin.

"But there is much worse in the sea, my dear barnacles. Here, let me show you one of my favorites."

She whistled as if she was calling a dog. Seconds later, a green-black dome, big enough to fill our living room back home, rose beneath us in a mass of bubbles. It lifted Shoal and me from the water on its leathery back. Looking down, I saw four massive fins, each the length of a surfboard, and a green scaly head shaped like that of a turtle. But the eyes gave it away. There was intelligence in them, and age. There was humanness. Sea turtles don't start out large. They grow slowly over years, over decades, and this one was enormous. It must be very old, and it must have seen a lot of really bad things.

"How may I serve you, mistress?" it asked in exactly the low, croaking voice you'd expect a sea turtle to speak with if the sea turtle was actually some poor slob who'd once been human.

"Take me to the Ferris wheel, pet," Skalla

commanded. "One last spell to cast, and then this will all be over."

The turtle started to swim, accompanied by Skalla's escort of sharks. How to stop her? Stab the turtle with my kelp-gardening implement? Skalla would only summon some other creature from the deep to transport her.

Maybe Shoal was right. Maybe I should just chuck Skalla as far as I could, or chop her head into firewood. My friends and I would still be doomed, but if there was a chance to stop her from drowning Los Huesos and ruling over a new Atlantis, it was worth it.

An L-shaped brass tube rose up in front of the turtle's path: a periscope. Then, in an eruption of bubbles that rivaled the turtle's, a spiral-shaped white seashell with red stripes surfaced. The size of an elephant, it gave off odors of motor oil and diesel fuel. With a determined frown, Trudy peered at us through a porthole of Griswald's death-trap submarine.

A hatch popped open on the top of the shell, and Shoal and I wasted no time. Shoal took a running leap across the turtle's back and flung herself at the hatch. I was right behind her.

"No!" Skalla roared.

There was a slow-motion moment when the turtle was no longer beneath my feet, when I was sailing across the distance between the turtle and the sub with nothing but ocean beneath me. And then, teeth.

Not a shark, but eels. Big ones, with teeth like ice picks. They had arms, and also hair, and their pointed snouts came at me like missiles.

The eels bit into the bottom of the pillowcase and tore open the fabric. The head fell free. I reached for it, putting my hand within range of those terrible, needle-lined mouths. My fingertips caught the tips of Skalla's stiff hair, but the eels had a better grip on her. They had her, and I caught Skalla's malevolent glare just before the turtle angled down into a steep dive. Left holding nothing but limp cloth, I climbed into the nautilus shell.

"Follow that turtle!" I shouted, securing the hatch after me.

Trudy sat on a bicycle banana seat before an array of controls, including a cassette tape deck and a built-in cigarette lighter. She threw a lever, her feet furiously spinning bike pedals. Behind her, on another seat, Shoal spun another pair of pedals, and there were yet more pedals and seats behind her. I hopped on and got to work.

"Hello, Trudy," said Shoal. "Thank you for coming to our rescue. But where did you obtain a submarine?"

"Back in the Shanghai tunnel. Once I saw Thatcher

go underwater, I figured I needed a way to go chase him, so I commandeered the nautilus. Griswald helped me launch it. He said it was built by one of the old Keepers."

"What happened to him?"

"Drowned in shallow water," said Trudy, peering through the porthole into the murk.

In the sub's dim headlight, I could just make out Skalla's head and the eels, still clinging to the back of the paddling turtle.

I told Trudy and Shoal what I'd learned about Skalla's scheme to rule over a new Atlantis, and that prompted us to pedal faster. The submarine groaned under the pressure of the depths. I tried not to pay too much attention to the water dribbling through the hatch seal.

"Hey," said Trudy. "I just noticed this button labeled *torpedo*."

"Press it!" Shoal shouted, with something like glee. "Here, I will do it!"

Trudy placed her hand protectively over the button. "Maybe we should know what it does first?"

"I presume it launches a torpedo," I offered helpfully.

"But how do we know it's not tipped with a thermonuclear warhead?"

"Because that kind of firepower would be awfully

ambitious for a giant nautilus shell powered by bicycle pedals? Besides, we're falling behind. Come on, this might be our only chance to catch the turtle."

Trudy gritted her teeth. "Okay, okay, I'm pressing it. I'm pressing a button, even though I don't know what it does, and hopefully I won't turn the whole continent into a smoking radioactive wasteland of—"

Shoal leaned forward and slammed her palm down on the button.

With a violent shudder, the submarine surged forward and we were hurtling along at great speed.

"Stop pedaling!" Trudy said, desperately grasping at the controls to stay on course.

But we weren't pedaling anymore. The submarine was under its own power now. We *were* the torpedo, and I figured we'd explode on impact with anything we struck.

The turtle came up fast in the porthole. Too fast.

"Trudy, watch out, we're going to—"

And we did. Crashed. Right into the giant's butt. The sub didn't so much explode as shatter, the shell walls cracking like an egg into thousands of tiny fragments. Water gushed in, and then the shell and the submarine were just more flotsam. Trudy, Shoal, and I followed a cascade of air bubbles to the surface.

A shark greeted us there.

"Howdy do," it said, lifting its face out of the

water. Its teeth looked like hatchet blades. "Swim with us to shore or we'll eat your legs."

Behind us, the sea turtle rose to the top of the choppy waters. Still riding on its back with her eels, Skalla was having herself a fine, horrific laugh.

CHAPTER 16

An army of Skalla's creatures waited for us on the beach in a drenching downpour. There were dozens and dozens of them: Lobster men and kelp guys and women with writhing eels for hair. There were manta rays with legs, their broad wings trailing awkwardly in the sand. There were lazily sprawled elephant seals wearing glasses, and five-limbed starfish smoking cigarettes, and little urchin children bristling with spines. And Tommy and Dicky, of course, the jellies. And the big sumo lobster from the Tunnel of Love.

With Skalla on its back, the turtle emerged from the surf and walked up the beach.

"You don't look much worse for the wear," said the witch. "That's good. I am pleased to see it. I'd hate for you to spill too much of your blood. It's quite precious to me."

"Why are you so . . . *nasty*?" I asked. "Was it too much junk food? Or just a lack of good adult role models?"

I was desperate to figure out what made her tick. If there was a chink in her armor, I needed to find it now.

"Isn't the answer obvious, little oyster? The king of Atlantis *cut off my head*. What more should it take to deserve my enmity? He took my body! Wouldn't you hate him if he'd done the same to you? Wouldn't you punish him for taking what can never be restored?"

I knew the answer. Of course I would hate him. Even if I'd deserved it, I'd hate him. But would that give me the right to respond with even more cruelty?

"But what about her?" I said, gesturing at Shoal. "And Trudy? What about all these people?" My gesture now encompassed her monstrous hybrids. "We didn't do anything to you."

I'd never seen Skalla smolder with more malice.

"Take them to the Ferris wheel," she spat. "And don't forget his kelp-gardening tool, and the girl's backpack."

One of the lobster men—the sumo—stripped Trudy

and me of our weapons, and with shoves and jabs from his bandaged claw, steered us to a cave opening in the cliffs. I'd have given anything for a pot of boiling water and a few pounds of butter.

Skalla's servants took us on a short march into a tunnel beneath the boardwalk, then up stairs carved out of sandstone. We emerged behind the construction fence surrounding the Ferris wheel. The wheel towered over us, a structure of algae green steel and rust with dangling bucket seats.

Murals decorated the backside of the construction fence. Similar to those in the Flotsam's summer palace, they depicted Atlantean history, but here the story was told from a different point of view. Here, Coriolis was a tyrant overseeing slaves. And Skalla was the hero, trying to liberate her people. She wore a brilliant blue skirt, like the color of the ocean on a sunny day. Sea horse tattoos curled around the long, lean muscles of her arms and legs. She wasn't exactly beautiful, but she was strong.

And something about those tattoos nagged at me.

I could still hear the waves smashing the shore like bombs. The air had gotten so damp, I felt as if I was a deep-sea diver, walking to my execution on the ocean floor. Things didn't feel like the regular world anymore. We'd crossed over into Skalla's territory.

Skalla rode up on her turtle to the edge of a trench

surrounding the Ferris wheel. "Behold, little clown fish," she said. "My new palace."

I looked up at the wheel. I looked all around the muddy grounds. "Seriously?" I asked.

"Look down, boy," said Skalla.

Lobsters pushed us closer to the rim of the trench, the big sumo giving me an extra hard shove. The trench went down a long way, at least as far as a mine shaft, maybe deeper. There was an entire world down there, the Ferris wheel just the cap of a tower plunging into the earth. Built of ocean-stained salvage— pieces that looked like parts of ships and bridges and oil-drilling platforms—the tower featured terraces and arches and catwalks. Scaffolding spiraled around the entire structure. Massive sea spiders with legs the size of construction cranes lifted girders and beams.

"I had the spiders outfit my tower with pontoons and stabilizers and sky-iron gyroscopes," Skalla said casually, like my dad talking about how he'd refurbished our bathroom. "Once my tidal wave strikes, we'll pull up anchor and float. There are engines too, and rudders, and cannons. I'll be able to take my city anywhere, to seek refuge, or to engage in conquest. It will be *good* to be queen." She waited a moment, as if we were supposed to applaud or something. When we didn't, she called out, "Let us launch my new era." Her voice echoed down the deep trench. The spiders below turned valves. Great jets of water thundered from pipes in the side of the pit.

Above us shrieked a devilish wind, drawing metallic groans from the Ferris wheel and rocking the bucket seats. Bodies spilled out from them, their falls arrested by cables fastened around their legs. The bodies swung in the wind. I recognized them.

"Father!" screamed Shoal.

Coriolis hung upside-down, along with Fin, and Concha the bike lady, and the guy who sold churros on the boardwalk, and the roller-coaster ticket taker— all of the Flotsam. And Griswald too. Skalla's creatures must have taken him while I was busy with the fish. He struggled, his face a bearded radish as blood rushed to his head.

"More water!" barked Skalla, and from the bottom of the pit came an enormous upswell of churning, foaming seawater. It was as if the only thing holding back the ocean had crumbled away, and now all the world's seas were rushing in. The water swirled in a furious whirlpool, faster and faster, the force so strong the ground shook. The steel supports of the Ferris wheel rattled, and the Atlanteans swung like piñatas.

With mud sliding beneath my feet, I almost slipped. And I learned something about lobsters then. Or at least about human abominations reshaped into lobsters. They're not so steady on two legs. Especially not lobsters the size of sumo wrestlers. My big guard went sprawling, and seeing my chance, I pounced. I dove on him and pummeled his face with both fists. Not that he felt it. But as he sloshed around in the mud, trying to stand, I snatched the kelp-gardening implement from his distracted claw and scrambled away.

Now all I needed to do was . . . what? Stab something? Poke something? The weather raged around us. This wasn't just a storm. This was Skalla preparing to drown Los Huesos and everything else for miles around.

"Kill her," Shoal entreated me.

I shook my head. "Even if I do, we'll all still be cursed."

"It doesn't matter anymore. She must not be allowed to extract her magic residue from us. She'll destroy *everything*."

Shoal was right.

Skalla had left us with no other choices.

I turned to her, my blade ready. Her creatures watched, waiting for her next order.

"Squid," said Skalla, calmly.

With a huge *sploosh*, a dusky red tentacle as thick as a telephone pole shot from the pit. Another followed, and both wrapped themselves around the lower struts of the Ferris wheel.

"Squiiiiiiiid!" I screamed.

Which seemed like an obvious thing to say, but I wasn't wrong. The tentacles belonged to a squid. A giant squid. A colossal squid. A monstrous, ginormous, seriously and insanely huge squid. Eight arms, each thicker than the first two tentacles, lifted from the water and curled around the Ferris wheel. The ride creaked and groaned as the beast hauled itself from the water and climbed up the spokes. Then an arrow-shaped head longer than a school bus emerged. Its parrotlike beak could have snapped a freeway in half. Of all Skalla's creatures, this was the most awful. Its eyes were gigantic but still human, complete with eyelashes.

My throat hurt, and I realized I'd been screaming for quite some time. I screamed even more when an arm lashed out and encircled my chest. I only stopped screaming when it cut off my air with a squeeze. Suction cups lined with teeth bit into my flesh. Through blood-hazed tunnel vision, I saw Trudy and Shoal getting the same treatment. The squid yanked us up high among the Ferris wheel's upper spokes, and I'd have puked if I hadn't been gripped so tight my innards couldn't move. I tried to free my sword hand, but it was no use.

Trudy struggled to get my attention. The squid's

arms had her by the chest and throat. "Muh," she gasped, turning blue. "Muhmmah! Heehorse!"

She was speaking the language of suffocation.

"Wah?" I answered back. Lack of oxygen had me seeing curtains of red. My head pounded with internal hammers.

From this high up I could see the entire boardwalk. Tourists ran screaming, though a few remained, staring up in dumb fascination. We'd get no help from them.

The wind tore gaps in the construction fence, sending plywood panels flying. A big piece helicoptered by me, depicting Coriolis's mistreatment of Skalla, the witch standing tall before his sword, her chin lifted proudly, her sea horse–tattooed arms tied behind her back.

There was something about those tattoos . . .

The witch's witchy cackle floated up to us, carried on wind and salt and spray. "Such a sweet sight. Just look at you, small fry, all strung up like cod on the smoking rack."

She snarled a command. From the whirlpool, sleek fish rocketed up at us in silver streaks. One passed close enough to brush my shoulder with the edge of its wing-fin. I felt nothing at first, but then a warm trickle ran down my arm: blood. Another fish gashed me over my eyebrow. They were like flying knives, circling me and my friends and the Flotsam, slicing our flesh. I watched my own blood dripping down, falling into the water.

I strained against the giant squid's arm as Skalla prepared to cast her final spell.

CHAPTER 17

Recoiling from the flying razor fish, I caught Trudy's eye. She was still trying to say something, but she was close to spent. So was Shoal. The three of us exchanged a look. I can't tell you what my friends were thinking, but I knew we shared something with that look, and I felt doomed but a little bit more brave.

Meanwhile, Griswald, hanging from a Ferris wheel seat above us, seemed to be choking. His throat produced a clucking little whine. It didn't sound human. It almost sounded like the keening cry of a . . . seagull?

A flying chaos of gray and white feathers slammedinto the squid's eyes: seagulls. The squid screamed with a bizarre, buzzing, squirting wail that sounded like the world's biggest malfunctioning toilet. Still gripping us all, its arms flailed, and we went wheeling through the air. It wasn't so bad, I tried to convince myself. It was just like a carnival ride: the Tilt-a-Squid.

Joking about it in my head that way *did* make it just the slightest bit more tolerable. At least it kept me from going out of my mind with misery and fear and defeat and barfing.

Distracted by the assault of beak and claw, the squid loosened its grip, just a little. I managed to wiggle one hand loose enough to yank at the suction cups biting into my opposite shoulder. My sword arm popped free, and I went berserk, chopping away with the kelp-gardening implement. Having already experienced chopping beyond my ability to chop, I knew I wouldn't fail. The squid's arm went limp, and I skidded down, digging my heels into its rubbery flesh to slow my descent and falling the last several feet into the soft mud at the foot of the Ferris wheel.

The gulls continued their battle with the squid and, amazingly, they seemed to be having an impact, like a bee swarm attacking a bear. The monster's tentacles began to sag, and Trudy and Shoal tumbled down its arms to land beside me. The squid whooshed its arms through the air in a vain attempt to ward off the birds. One by one, *thwop* by *thwop*, it pulled its suction cups off the Ferris wheel struts until it wasn't holding on to anything, and the great cephalopod plummeted into the whirlpool with a mighty splash.

Drenched, panting, and cut, Shoal and Trudy and I helped one another to our feet. Trudy didn't look good at all. A huge sucker mark bruised her throat, and her lips were blue.

"Muhmmuh," she said, her eyes wide.

Shoal and I held her steady and told her not to try to speak. But that just agitated her even more.

"Heeorse!"

Just a few yards from where we'd landed, Skalla's head sat atop her turtle. She didn't look enraged. She didn't look upset. She looked happy.

"You failed, little plankton. Failed to stop me. Failed to save your fellow Flotsam. First I'll wash away Los Huesos. I'll drown San Francisco. And Santa Cruz. And Monterey and Carmel and Pismo and Los Angeles and San Diego. I'll wash away anything I please and replace it with a kingdom more to my liking." Her eyes had gone dark and heavy as magnets, and when she spoke again, her voice wasn't human, as if the words were coming out sideways. Feathers, saltwater, and blood flew on the wind.

At the horizon rose a mountain of water. The

churning wave boiled with all the energy of an earthquake, a tornado, a hurricane, a nuclear bomb, rushing toward us.

We had lost. It was over.

I turned toward my friends one last time. I wanted
to say good-bye but my tongue froze in my mouth.
Something had caught my attention. At my feet lay
wreckage from the construction fence, a board with
part of a mural of Skalla. Just one of her arms. Long
and brown, decorated with sea horses.

"Heeorse!" Trudy coughed. "Muhmmmah!"

And I got it.

With the tidal wave's cold shadow blanketing my
shoulders, I said, "Call it off. I know what you need."

There was murder in Skalla's eyes.

"Call it off," I said again, "and I'll give you back
your body."

CHAPTER 18

Skalla halted the wave.

It loomed like a skyscraper, curling over us, rippling like a monumental slab of Jell-O. The flying fish soared in wide circles around Griswald and the hanging Flotsam. Gulls wheeled overhead but didn't cry.

"What did you say?" Her whisper was low and dangerous. If she decided to let the wave go, everything around would be crushed to splinters and slop, including us.

I pointed at the board from the construction fence. "I remember where I've seen those sea horse tattoos." Trudy nodded triumphantly. "I know where your body is. I can take you to it."

Skalla's withered lips moved. The tidal wave above shimmered.

"Why would I care?"

"Because your wave will destroy your body too." I waited while she calculated.

"Show me," Skalla said.

"Free the Flotsam and Griswald first."

"This isn't a negotiation, boy!" Skalla roared. "Take me to my body or I'll let my wave pound you down to the center of the Earth."

Shoal stepped forward, her fingers curled into fists. "Don't give her anything, Thatcher. Not until she frees my family."

Trudy nodded in vigorous agreement.

Skalla stared straight at me, unblinking.

"Better decide, sand flea. I won't keep my wave frozen forever."

How could I trust her? What if I gave Skalla her body back and she still drowned everything? How did this decision ever fall on me? What a stupid summer vacation.

"Follow me," I said.

Skalla left most of her creatures behind to guard the Flotsam, but a contingent of lobster men flanked us as her sea turtle sloshed down the flooded boardwalk to Griswald's museum. Her chin cut through the saturated air like the figurehead of a pirate ship.

Sinbad hissed at us from atop a display cabinet

when we entered the museum. The storm had shattered the windows, tossing things around like soggy confetti and flooding the whole place a foot deep. Shards of shattered exhibit jars littered the shelves. The octopus with sneakers cowered in a corner. The shrunken heads bobbed like apples in the water, moaning with dread. The sodden air smelled like cat pee and fish puke. But the mummy's sarcophagus was still in its place, resting on its sawhorses.

Like Skalla's head, Griswald had found the mummy washed up on the beach. He hadn't known what he was keeping in his museum. Maybe he'd never seen pictures of a whole-bodied Skalla with her sea horse tattoos.

Would my plan work? Offering Skalla her body back was one thing, but once she saw the condition it was in, would she even want such a shriveled, mildewy piece of wreckage?

"Show it to me," Skalla commanded.

I lifted the lid open and one of Skalla's lobsters carried her over and angled her head above the mummy. She stared at it for what seemed like hours.

"Thatcher, give me your blade," Shoal hissed at me. "If you won't kill her, let me."

With her hand on her throat, Trudy nodded.

Maybe they were right. Maybe I was just making things worse.

But when I saw a single tear trace a path down Skalla's chalky white cheek, I knew I'd made the right decision, no matter how things ultimately turned out.

"It's my body," Skalla said at last. "I thought it was lost with the island-city. But it's me. I could have my body back. I could walk on two legs. Swim through the waves like a porpoise. Be strong. Whole."

She didn't seem to know or care that the rest of us were still in the room with her. But I needed to snap her back to reality. What if she forgot the only thing keeping the tidal wave at bay was her magical will? I could feel it, like a gigantic fist cocked back and ready to smash.

I shut the lid of the sarcophagus. "Call off your wave. Free the Atlanteans and Griswald. Remove the curse. Then you can have your body back."

The sumo lobster man's antennae twitched, and I remembered what he'd said in the Tunnel of Love. I remembered Tommy and Dicky and their grand-mother and Zoltan.

"And restore your creatures to the way they were," I added. "Tommy and Dicky and the kelp guys. And the Keepers too. All of them."

The sea turtle nodded approvingly.

Skalla coughed. "I'll try."

🐚

Skalla's gaze landed on me, then Trudy, then Shoal, and then back to me, as if standing in her glare somehow marked us. "Your heart pumps seawater," she said. "The sound you hear when you cup your ears is the ancient ocean tide. The ocean is the bloodstream of the world. Stir the pot and the sea responds." She drew breath through her withered lips. "Now, fill the sarcophagus."

Using a salad bowl I found floating in the hallway, I scooped water into the sarcophagus until it leaked through the seams. The mummy floated like a sliver of soap. Under Skalla's direction, we weighed it down with dumbbells from Griswald's bedroom.

"It will suffice," Skalla said, supervising. "Now, put me in."

I took her head from the lobster man and gladly dunked her under the water. Her eyes remained open. Bubbles dribbled from the corner of her mouth. I let go of her head and watched her sink.

Then . . . nothing.

The room grew quiet. I heard my own breathing, and Sinbad's purr, and plinking drips all around the flooded museum, steady as clockwork. Outside, the vertical ocean roared and gloshed.

Then, several things happened at the same time:

The water in the sarcophagus turned gray white, like skim milk, the color of Skalla's face.

Every lightbulb in the museum exploded in a puff of glass.

My ears popped.

Thunder boomed, rattling the windows.

Sinbad coughed up a hairball.

The hairball didn't have anything to do with Skalla's magic, as far as I knew.

The witch's nose broke the surface, followed by her chin, and then the rest of her face. Her lips moved as she said something too low to hear. I leaned over the edge of the sarcophagus to get closer.

"It didn't work," she croaked. "I don't have enough magic in me."

"That's not our fault," I protested. "We did everything you told us to."

Her eyelids closed heavily. "Not enough."

"I knew she would have an excuse," Shoal said. Her voice was like ice. "Let me kill her."

"If we kill her, we lose," I said. "The wave comes down. The curse remains. All her monsters stay monsters. Thousands die."

"But at least then she won't rule a counterfeit Atlantis," said Shoal. "Her crimes must stop here. We must stop the tide forever."

We were both right.

I raised the Atlantean blade. My face stared back at me, reflected in the volcanic glass.

And I slid the edge of the blade across my palm. It hurt worse than I thought it would, and bled more. Wincing, I let the magic stream into the sarcophagus.

"Thatcher, no!" screamed Trudy.

I gently shoved her away.

"Leave me alone, Trudy."

"You'll bleed to death!"

"She doesn't have enough magic," I explained. "But there's still some of it left in me. If I give it back, maybe it'll be enough."

I would give the witch as much as she needed, all of it, if that's what it took. As long as she used the magical soup ingredient to save the town and save my friends, I'd accept anything that happened to me. And that's what I was thinking as I started to feel light-headed. That's what I was thinking when my vision went watery and closed down to a tighter and tighter tunnel of black. I was still thinking it when Trudy and Shoal eased me to the floor.

I wanted to keep bleeding into the sarcophagus, but I was too weak to shove Trudy and Shoal off and get back to the very important work of bleeding.

"Go into the bathroom and bring me first aid supplies," Trudy barked at the sumo lobster, and I guess he did what she told him because after a fuzzy moment when I must have faded out, Trudy was wrapping my hand in gauze.

"Ow," I said with numb lips. "Hurts."

"Of course. Tourniquets hurt. Dummy."

"More magic," I said. "She needs more."

Trudy fastened her knot.

"Ow," I said again.

"You're brave and funny when you're not getting on my nerves. And also smart, even though you're dumb."

She watched me until I could sit up on my own, and then she took my blade. With a quick intake of breath, she cut her own palm and bled into the water.

She bled for a very long time.

A while later, Shoal took the kelp-gardening implement from her. She stared down at the witch. Her eyes glittered. Tension drew her narrow face into a tight mask. The witch had taken so much from her, and if Shoal didn't want to give her magic but decided to drive the blade right between her eyes, I wouldn't blame her.

Instead, Shoal sliced open her palm.

Standing together in pain, my friends turned the water red.

CHAPTER 19

And so, at the end of summer, I went home. My parents met me at the airport in Phoenix. They gave me a T-shirt from Singapore. It said, "My parents went to Singapore and they didn't even get this T-shirt from there." They thought it was hilarious.

On the first day of school my new English teacher made us write an essay about our summer vacations. I wrote down everything, exactly the way it happened.

I wrote how Skalla rose from the mummy's sarcophagus, her eyes gleaming like sunlight on the sea. The sumo lobster man offered a claw to help her out, but she waved him off and climbed out by herself. She was young, the way she must have looked before Coriolis cut off her head. She was whole.

Unaccustomed to having her head attached to her body, she wobbled on her feet, but it didn't take her long to find her balance. I gave her a Los Huesos souvenir T-shirt and a beach towel to wear as a skirt, and that's how she walked out of Griswald's museum. We followed her, terrified that she'd let her wave annihilate the town. If she spoke anything that sounded like magic, I swore I'd take her head right back off.

The fog clotted, thick as mashed potatoes, and I lost sight of her. Frantically, Trudy, Shoal, and I searched through the fog. But after a few minutes, I knew she was gone.

I felt like an empty grocery bag. Lifeless. Drained of more than just blood.

"I should have known," I said. "I should have found a way to force her. I should have—"

Shoal put a hand on my shoulder. "It is not your fault, Thatcher. You did everything you could . . ."

She didn't finish her sentence. The fog cleared, as if sucked into the sky by a giant vacuum cleaner. Sun shined down from a blue sky.

Skalla was still nowhere in sight.

But neither was her tidal wave.

"She actually did it," said the sumo lobster, dancing down the boardwalk. He was no longer a lobster man. Now he was just a really big guy with a buzz cut and an I ♥ Los Huesos T-shirt. He looked like a three-year-old about to blow out the candles on his birthday cake. "Look at me!" he shouted gleefully. "I'm not a stupid fish! I'm a guy! A man! A dude!"

"Technically speaking, you were never a fish," Trudy said. "Lobsters are crustaceans."

"Okay! Whatever! Okay! Hey, I committed a lot of crimes in this town, so I am out of here!" And he took off laughing.

As we hurried down the boardwalk toward the Ferris wheel, we encountered big men with dreadlocks. Pointy-featured guys smoking cigarettes. And Tommy and Dicky, popping wheelies on their bikes with their pale but very human faces tilted skyward to bask in the sun.

The boardwalk was crowded with people blinking in the bright light, some looking confused, some looking fearful, but many of them relieved and happy. A short man rubbed his eyes. He was wearing trousers made of fish and was speaking excitedly to a trio of men with small, but not quite shrunken, heads.

And there was a red-faced girl with deep scratches marking her bare arms. I caught her shy look and she turned her head, but I'd already recognized her by her eyes.

"Hey," I said, approaching her.

"Hey," she said, not looking at me.

"I'm sorry about your arms."

She rubbed her scratches. "It's okay. They're already healing. I'm sorry I squeezed you so tight."

"It's okay. You were a squid."

"Yeah."

We stood in awkward silence, and she threw her arms around me in a rush. Even as a regular girl, she had an amazing grip.

"Thanks," she said, and she ran off before I could get too sniffly.

Farther down the boardwalk, we found Griswald, bewildered and completely soaked, but alive. One of his feet was still inside his big, clomping boot. The pink toes of the other poked out from the bottom of his pant leg. He wiggled them. And looked sad.

"If Skalla's restored all my exhibits to their former state, I guess the museum's out of business," he said.

"I think you can probably buy freaks on the Internet."

He considered this a moment before breaking out in a broad smile. "You know, that's not a bad idea. I could branch out into three-headed chickens and UFO babies. Besides, the sea always bestows wonders. Ever find a piece of sea glass in the sand, all polished round and smooth? One out of every thousand pieces of sea glass came from the very first Atlantis. Think about that."

Skalla had healed his foot, but maybe not his brain. Maybe not all the way. Or maybe she had, but Griswald was just fundamentally a strange person. And maybe that was okay.

I turned to my friends and noticed the expression on Shoal's face. She wasn't happy. She was scared. Terrified.

"My family," Shoal said to Griswald. "Did Skalla . . . ? Are they . . . ?"

And, yes, apparently Skalla had, because the Flotsam came toward us, covered in bandages, but alive.

Shoal jumped into Coriolis's waiting arms, and watching them embrace warmed me like a mug of hot cocoa, complete with whipped cream and an extra drizzle of chocolate syrup.

Fin and Concha the bike lady came up to me and Trudy. Concha looked down at us, her face a stern mask.

"You gave the witch her body back."

"Yeah."

"And now she can do everything she did before. She can rest and brew her magic until she's ready to strike again. And next time, she'll be doing it on two legs."

"Maybe she doesn't need that anymore," Trudy said.

Fin chewed his lip. "I suppose we'll see. If the sea

calls us back again at the end of summer and we find ourselves trudging across the beach, letting ourselves sink into the waves and fall into the Drowning Sleep—"

"The tide pulls at the earth," Coriolis said. "It tugs the sand. It reclaims stone and wood. The sea is relentless. It reaches with greedy fingers, and one day it *will* reclaim this entire beach. Yes, it will take the boardwalk, and Los Huesos, and all of California. And the lands beyond that. Eventually, the sea welcomes everyone back to her cold, churning embrace." He smiled down at us, squinting in the sunlight. "But not, I hope, for a very, very long time."

§

My essay was really good. It was thorough. And I got a zero on it because I never turned it in. The only people who wouldn't accuse me of making it all up were hundreds of miles from me.

The school year went on. I took thirty-three math quizzes. I did six book reports. I memorized and forgot all the Articles of the Constitution.

Internet and phone access in Los Huesos still stank, so I exchanged a grand total of 174 letters and postcards with Trudy and Shoal.

I thought about signing up for tae kwon do again,

but I found a different school where they taught kung fu. I liked it there. It was good to start fresh. I wasn't very good at it, but that wasn't important. Every time I did a push-up, I thought about Trudy, training herself to be a superhero/detective. Every time I struck the punching bag, I thought about Shoal, relentless and fierce.

My parents were worried about me. They said I was acting strangely. They sent me to talk to the school counselor. I admitted I'd had a weird summer vacation but that I'd made good friends and I missed them and Phoenix didn't feel right. Phoenix wasn't the same because the world wasn't the same. There were witches and monsters in it, but also superheroes and princesses from lost cities.

I didn't tell anyone about the specifics.

Around February I started begging my parents to let me spend another summer with Griswald. Now they knew for sure there was something wrong with me. But by June, they'd surrendered.

On the last day of school, when the final bell rang, my suitcase was waiting for me on my bed when I got home. I'd packed it before breakfast. My folks drove me to the airport, and just a few hours later I was standing amid the stink of kelp on the sand-flea-infested beach of Los Huesos.

Trudy had grown an inch. Her biceps were bigger than mine. Shoal looked about the same. She wore a Barracudas Swim Team sweatshirt. The Barracudas were the mascots of Los Huesos Middle School. Trudy had been helping Shoal catch up on land-dweller things, such as algebra.

In some ways, Los Huesos was even a little weirder than before. People thought the colossal wave from last summer had something to do with global warming. And as for the monster squid and other oddities, surely eyewitnesses had gotten carried away in their descriptions. Scientists were studying the place. And the Atlanteans were making money by selling the scientists T-shirts and non-nutritious snacks. They used the money to convert Skalla's Ferris wheel tower palace into an attraction: New Atlantis. Adult admission was four bucks, and people were paying it. One day, it would be a true Atlantis, and a good one.

We stood on the sand together, Trudy and Shoal and I, staring out at the sea. The waves came and went, came and went. I figured I'd also be coming and going. To and from my friends, maybe for the next few years, maybe for the rest of my life. Wherever I went and whatever I did, a part of me had washed up on these shores, and I'd always leave a part of me behind.

We stayed on the beach a long time, being close, feeling right.

After a while, I couldn't stand it anymore.

"I swear if we don't get a pizza right now, I am going to die."

Trudy and Shoal punched me. It hurt, and I laughed.

ACKNOWLEDGMENTS

I had a bajillion people help me in various ways with this book, and I guarantee I'm going to forget to thank some of them, so, really, what's the point in thanking *any* of them? Okay, okay, I'll try, but I'll have to apologize in advance to those whose generous assistance goes unacknowledged here. I'll make it up to you, I swear.

From the Blue Heaven 2008 writers workshop: Paolo Bacigalupi, Tobias Buckell, Sarah K. Castle, Deborah Coates, C. C. Finlay, Daryl Gregory, Sandra McDonald, Paul Melko, Jenn Reese, and Catherynne M. Valente. And a particularly ginormous blob of thanks goes to Sarah Prineas, for her constant support and smartitude.

Gooey thanks as well go to Tim Pratt and Heather Shaw. And, as ever, to Lisa Will.

I'm also grateful to the awesome Caitlin Blasdell, who navigates me through the tricky waters of the publishing business, and to my editor, Margaret Miller, and her colleagues, who turned a thick stack of my incoherent ramblings into the book you now hold in your hands.

Finally, a nod to Steve at the Museum of the Weird in Austin, Texas, where I spent part of a pleasant afternoon perusing his displays of wonderfully disgusting things. Best three bucks I ever spent.

052559748